08-CFD-913

D0348532

THE PE̶R̶F̶E̶C̶T̶

''Why must you always be so damnably perfect?''

Pierre didn't so much as blink. ''What would you like me to say, Caroline? This perfection you speak of is my personal curse, but I did not mean to inflict it on you. I should be willing to do anything to oblige you.''

Looking up at him consideringly, she gave in to impulse and raised a hand, deliberately mussing the front of his hair. ''There,'' she said. ''You look almost human, Pierre. Now I believe I can do justice to my dinner.''

She took one step toward the dining room before Pierre's hand snaked out and pulled her back. Without a word, he hauled her into his arms and kissed her, hard and long and quite thoroughly.

Other Regency Romances by
Kasey Michaels
From Avon Books

THE BELLIGERENT MISS BOYNTON
THE LURID LADY LOCKPORT
THE MISCHIEVOUS MISS MURPHY
THE PLAYFUL LADY PENELOPE
THE QUESTIONING MISS QUINTON
THE RAMBUNCTIOUS LADY ROYSTON
THE SAVAGE MISS SAXON
THE TENACIOUS MISS TAMERLANE

By Loretta Chase
THE ENGLISH WITCH
ISABELLA

By Joanna Harris
WORLDLY INNOCENT

Coming Soon

VISCOUNT VAGABOND
by Loretta Chase

Avon Books are available at special quantity discounts for bulk
purchases for sales promotions, premiums, fund raising or edu-
cational use. Special books, or book excerpts, can also be created
to fit specific needs.

For details write or telephone the office of the Director of Special
Markets, Avon Books, Dept. FP, 105 Madison Avenue, New
York, New York 10016, 212-481-5653.

THE
ANONYMOUS
MISS ADDAMS

KASEY MICHAELS

AVON BOOKS  NEW YORK

THE ANONYMOUS MISS ADDAMS is an original publication of Avon Books. This work has never before appeared in book form. This work is a novel. Any similarity to actual persons or events is purely coincidental.

AVON BOOKS
A division of
The Hearst Corporation
105 Madison Avenue
New York, New York 10016

Copyright © 1989 by Kathie Seidick
Published by arrangement with the author
Library of Congress Catalog Card Number: 89-91300
ISBN: 0-380-75668-4

All rights reserved, which includes the right to reproduce this book or portions thereof in any form whatsoever except as provided by the U.S. Copyright Law. For information address Cantrell-Colas, Inc., 229 East 79th Street, New York, New York 10021.

First Avon Books Printing: November 1989

AVON TRADEMARK REG. U.S. PAT. OFF. AND IN OTHER COUNTRIES, MARCA REGISTRADA, HECHO EN U.S.A.

Printed in the U.S.A.

RA 10 9 8 7 6 5 4 3 2 1

To Ellen Edwards, who patiently midwifed
the longest labor in publishing history.
Thanks, friend!

Prologue

"And I say she has to die! Damn it, can't you see? Haven't you been forever telling me that she has to go? It's the only way out, for both of us!"

"Not necessarily. You could always marry her," a female voice suggested. "You'd make a wonderfully handsome groom. And, please, my dearest, don't swear."

"Marry her? *Marry her!* Are you daft? Have you been sipping before noon again? How many times must I tell you? I'd druther shackle m'self to an ox—it would be easier to haul a dumb animal to the altar. Besides, the chit don't like me, not even above half."

"Can't hold that against the girl. You never were so popular as I'd like."

"That's nothing to the point! We're talking about her now. The only answer is to do away with her."

"All right, be bloodthirsty if you must. Boys will be boys. That leaves only the question—who and how do we handle disposing of the wretched girl?"

"That's two questions. I don't know *how* to do it, but I do know *who*. I've thought this out most carefully. We both do the deed. That way neither of us is apt to cry rope on the other."

There was a short silence while his co-conspirator weighed his latest suggestion. "You really believe that I'd be so mean-spirited as to lay information against my own—oh, all right. Don't pout, it makes nasty lines around your mouth. We both do it. Now—*how* do we do it?"

"An accident. It should look like an accident. The best murders are always made to look like accidents."

1

"That does leave out poison, firearms, and a rope, doesn't it? Pity. I do so favor poison. It's so neat and reliable. A fall, perhaps? From the top of the tower? No, on second thought, that would be too messy. Think of the time we'd have cleaning the cobblestones. I suppose we must find another way."

"A riding accident, perhaps."

"That's brilliant! You were always so creative. A riding accident is perfect! She's always out and about somewhere on that terrible brute she rides. I'm more than surprised she hasn't snapped her neck a dozen times already, more's the pity that she hasn't. All right, a riding accident it is. Now, when do we do the deed?"

"She reaches her majority the tenth of October. The ninth ought to do it."

"That's cutting it a slice too fine, even for such a brilliant mind as yours. Something could go amiss and we wouldn't have time for a second chance. I would rather do it the first of the month. That way we won't have to waste any of her lovely money on birthday presents."

"Yes, why should we throw good money away on—I say! What was that?"

"Where?"

"Over there, behind the shrubbery. I saw something move. Blast it all, someone's been listening! Look! She's running away. Let me pass. I've got to catch her before she ruins everything!"

"Be careful of your breeches!" his companion cried after him. "This is only the second time you've worn them."

Chapter One

It was a room into which sunlight drifted, light-footedly skimming across the elegant furnishings, its brightness filtered by the gossamer-thin ivory silk curtains that floated at the tall windows.

The ceiling was also ivory, its stuccoed perimeter artfully molded into wreaths of flowers caught up by ram's heads, with dainty arabesques and marching lines of husks terminating in ribbon knots, while the walls had been painted by Cipriani himself and boasted tastefully romping nymphs, liquid-eyed goddesses, and a few doting *amorini.*

The furniture boasted the straight, clean lines of the brothers Adams—Robert and James—the dark, gilded mahogany vying with painted Wedgwood colors and the elegant blue and white satin striping of the upholstery.

To the awestruck observer, the entire room was a soul-soothing showplace, an exemplary example of the degree of refined elegance possible in an extraordinarily beautiful English country estate.

To Pierre Claghorn Standish, just then pacing the length of the Aubusson carpet, it was home.

"Oh, do sit down, Pierre," a man's voice requested wearily. "It's most fatiguing watching you prowl about the place like some petulant caged panther. I say panther because they are black, you know. Must you always wear that funereal color? It's really depressing. You remind me of an ink blot, marring the pristine perfection of my lovely blue and white copybook. It's jarring; upon my soul, it is. Look at me, for instance. This new green coat of mine is subdued, yet it whispers of life, of hope, of the glorious promise of spring. You look like the dead of winter—a very long, depressingly hard winter."

Pierre ceased pacing to look at his father, who was sitting at his ease, his elbows propped on the arms of his chair, his long fingers spread wide apart and steepled as he gazed up at his son. "Ah," André Standish said, his handsome face lighting as he smiled. "I do believe I have succeeded in gaining your attention. How wonderful. I shall have to find some small way in which to reward myself. Perhaps a new pony for my stables? But to get back to the point. You have been here for three days, my son, visiting your poor, widowed father in his loneliness— a full two days longer than any of your infrequent visits to me in the past five years, seven months, and six days. I think we can safely assume the formalities have been dutifully observed. Do you not believe it is time for you to get to the point?"

Pierre looked at his father and saw himself as he would appear in thirty years. The man had once been as dark as he, although now his hair was nearly all silver, but his black eyes still flashed brightly in his lean, deeply tanned face. His body was still firmly muscled, thanks to an active, sporting life, and he had not given one inch to his advancing years. Pierre smiled, for he could do a lot worse than follow in his father's footsteps.

"What makes you think there is anything to discuss?" Pierre asked, lowering himself into the chair facing his father. "Perhaps you are entering into your dotage and are only imagining things. Have you entertained that possibility, Father?"

André regarded him levelly. "I would rather instead reflect on the grave injustice I have done you by not beating you more often during your youth," he answered cheerfully. "You may be the scourge of London society, Pierre, if the papers and my correspondence are to be believed, but you are naught but a babe in arms when it comes to trying to fence with me, your sire and one-time mentor. Now, if you have been unable to discover a way onto the subject, may I suggest that you begin by telling me all about the funeral of that dastardly fellow, Quennel Quinton? After all, he's been below ground feeding the worms for more than three months.''

Only by the slight lifting of one finely sculpted eyebrow did Pierre Standish acknowledge that his father had surprised him by landing a flush hit. "Very good, Father," he complimented smoothly. "My congratulations to your network of spies. Perhaps you'd like to elaborate and tell me what I'm about to say next?''

André sighed and allowed his fingers to intertwine, lightly laying his chin on his clasped hands. "Must I, Pierre? It's all so mundane. Oh, very well. We could start with the box, I suppose.''

Now Pierre couldn't contain his surprise. His eyes widened, and he leaned forward in his chair, gripping the armrests. "You *know?*" he questioned dumbly, as nothing more profound came to his lips.

André rose to go over to the drinks cabinet—an elegant piece containing several delicately carved shelves and holding a generous supply of assorted spirits—and took his time debating over just which crystal decanter held exactly the proper drink for the moment. "Yes," he said consideringly, finally selecting a deep burgundy and pouring generous amounts into two glasses, "I rather think this will do.'' Returning to his chair, he held out one glass to his son. "Here you go, Pierre. Red with meat—and confession. Rather apt, don't you think? And close your mouth, if you please. It's decidedly off-putting.''

Pierre took the glass, automatically raising it to his lips, then shook his head as he watched André gracefully lower his body once more into the chair. "Much as I know you abhor hearing someone tell you what you already know, Father, I must say this out loud so that I can believe it. You knew Quennel Quinton was blackmailing Anton Follet? You knew the box left to me in Quinton's will was full of love letters Follet had written to—had written to—''

"My wife," André finished neatly. "Dearest Eleanore, your mother, to mimic you and likewise point out the obvious. Yes, of course I knew. Quinton first tried to blackmail me with those silly letters, but I convinced him of the futility of that particular course and suggested he apply to Follet instead. Follet's wife holds the purse strings, you understand. I imagine the poor fellow was put through hoops these past half-dozen years, sniffing about everywhere for the money to keep Quinton quiet. Why, the economies he must have been forced to endure! I do seem to remember hearing something about the man having to sell up most of his hunting stock at Tatt's. But then, one must pay the piper if one is going to commit things to paper. You'll remember, Pierre, that I always warned you against just that sort of foolishness.''

It was taking some time for his father's words to sink into Pierre's brain, and even then he missed the significance of the words ''silly letters.'' ''Quinton approached me within two months of arriving here after being invalided home from Spain, to learn that Mother had died. He waved the letters in front of me as he smiled—quite gleefully, I recall—and told me of Mother's romantic indiscretion, then said I would have to pay for his silence.''

''Wasn't very smart, this man Quinton, was he? I'm astounded that he stayed above ground as long as he did.''

Pierre laughed, a short, dissatisfied chuckle. ''No, he was not very smart. I entertained the notion of ridding the world of the man, but rejected the idea as needlessly exertive. As you said, Father, I am your student, as well as adverse to being blackmailed. In the end, I, too, suggested he apply to Follet for funds, with the stipulation that he leave me the letters in his will so that I might continue the blackmail myself. After all, Mother was dead. I needed to take my revenge somewhere.'' Pierre allowed his gaze to shift toward the carpet. ''I didn't go through with my intention, I must admit, but it seemed a reasonably workable idea at the time. I was rather overset.''

''Oh, Pierre, let's not dress the matter up in fine linen. You were devastated! Otherwise, you would have repeatedly beaten Quinton about the head until he gave the damning letters over to you. You felt betrayed, by your mother and then by me, whom you felt must have been a dismal failure as a husband if my wife had been forced to seek love elsewhere. You stormed off to London in a childish snit and have returned here only sporadically ever since, duty calls to your aging father. Isn't that right, Pierre?''

Suddenly Pierre was angry. Very angry. He jumped up from his chair and stalked over to the window, to look out over the perfectly manicured gardens. ''What did you expect me to do? Confront you? I had left here to fight on the Continent believing that you and Mother were the perfect couple. It certainly was the impression you gave. Then, shortly after I returned home, injured and weary, I learned that my sainted mother had not only died, but left behind her a legacy of shame and disgrace. I couldn't in good conscience intrude on your grief by telling you about it, yet at the same time I was angry with you for forcing her to indulge herself with someone like Follet. I had to get away before I exploded.''

It was quiet in the room for a few minutes, during which time the Standish butler entered and looked to his master for instructions concerning the serving of the evening meal, only to be waved closer so that he could hear a short, whispered instruction.

André Standish allowed his son time to compose himself, then walked over to place a hand on Pierre's shoulder. ''Have you read Follet's searing love missives, my son, now that they are at last in your possession?'' he asked, his voice light. ''Or have you thought to tell me about them at last and then burn them, unread, like some brainless ninny out of a very bad pennypress novel?''

''No, I hadn't thought of burning them,'' Pierre answered, slowly gaining control of himself. He felt off balance, a feeling to which he was unaccustomed, and he disliked the sensation immensely. In London he was respected, even feared. Here, he was once again his father's son, standing in awe of the master. ''Nor have I read them. I couldn't bring myself that low. To be truthful, I don't know what I plan to do with them. That's why I'm here—

7

prowling about your drawing room like a panther. What I don't know is what you hope to gain by dragging this old scandal out for an airing.''

"Here you are, sir.''

André turned to take the wooden box from the butler. "Thank you, Hartley. You are obedience itself. You may retire now. See that we are not disturbed.''

"Very good, sir. Thank you, sir,'' the butler agreed, backing from the room, closing the double doors behind him as he went.

Pierre turned his head to see the offending box, then once more directed his gaze toward the gardens. "Taken to burgling my rooms, have you, Father? I am discovering new, disturbing things about you with each passing moment. I don't want to hear those letters read, if that's what you have in mind. How could you read them and still retain any feeling for Mother?''

"Quite easily, I imagine,'' André replied, opening the box and picking up at random one of the dozen or so letters. "I loved Eleanore very much, Pierre, and miss her more with each passing day. Oh, my, there seems to be the smell of old perfume about these letters. Follet was always the fop, as I remember. No wonder that servant I turned off for attempting to steal some of your dear mother's possessions took them posthaste to Quinton. Let's see, I think I can make out this dreadful chicken scrawl. Oh, the spelling! It's ludicrous! I'm afraid I must deny your request and read this one aloud. Prepare yourself, my son.''

André made a short business of clearing his throat and then began to read. " 'My dearest dimpled darling, light of my deepest heart.' '' He closed his eyes for a moment. "Oh, that is dreadful, isn't it? I can barely read on but, for your sake, Pierre, I shall persevere. 'I sat awake till the wee morning hours just before dawn, my celestial love, thinking of you and our hasty, beatific meeting in the enchanted gardens last night. How I long to tell you all that is in my love-besieged heart, all the wonder and glory that I feel for you, but there seems no way we can escape for long your dastardly husband, André.' Oh, that is good,''

André stopped to comment. "He used my name—just in case it had slipped your mother's mind, I suppose. No wonder Eleanore kept the letters; they're better than a night at Covent Garden."

"That is sufficient, thank you. You may stop there," Pierre cut in, disgusted with his father's levity. "Isn't it enough that she had an affair with the man? Must you read his reminiscences of it?"

"An affair?" André repeated, his voice suddenly very cold, very hard. "You insolent pup! How dare you! Haven't you heard a word I've read? The man was—is—an ass. A total ass! If his harridan of a wife hadn't hauled him off to Ireland, you would have discovered that for yourself. Do you really mean to stand there and tell me you still believe someone as wonderful, as intelligent as your mother would have given the idiot who wrote this drivel so much as the time of day? Why do you think I didn't kill Quinton when he first approached me? I laughed him out of the house!"

Pierre slowly turned away from the window to look piercingly at his father. "Are you telling me Follet's love was all one-sided?"

André smiled. "Ah, and to think for a moment there I was beginning to believe you were slow. Yes, Pierre, Follet's all-consuming passion for your mother was very much one-sided. To be perfectly frank, as I remember it, Eleanore considered him to be a toad. A particularly slimy toad." He tipped his head to one side, as if reliving some private memory. "I readily recall one evening—Follet was skipping about our first-floor balcony at the London town house reciting some terrible love poem he had written to her pert nose, or some such nonsense, and causing no end of racket—until your mother cut him off by dousing him with a pitcher of cold water."

Pierre smiled wanly, then returned to the drinks table to refill his glass. "All this time, wasted." He turned to his father. "If you knew what I was thinking all these years—and how you knew I shall not be so silly as to ask, considering that you know everything—why didn't you tell me? All these long years I've been warring with myself, trying to banish my love for my mother, trying to understand how human beings can be so fickle, so devious. And you knew—you knew!''

André put his arm around his son. "I must confess, I have known the whole truth for less than two years. It took me that long to figure out the reason for your defection, as I had taught you to hide your tracks very successfully. I had thought to tell you the truth then, but deep inside I was just the least bit put out that you could believe Quinton's obvious lies, and I made up my mind to wait until you came to your senses. And, never fear, you never stopped loving your mother. I see the flowers you order placed on her grave every week, and I've watched you when you visit the cemetery.

"But I've also watched you grow and mature these past years, even more than you did during your years with me, or your time spent on the Peninsula. You have become a devoted student of human nature, my son, taking all that I've taught you and honing it to a fine edge. Of course, you have become a shade too arrogant, and even, dare I say it, a bit cold—but I think we can safely assume that your arrogance has now suffered a healing setback.''

"This has all been in the way of a *lesson?*" Pierre asked, incredulous. "I can't believe it.''

"Oh, dear,'' André remarked, looking at his son. "You're angry, aren't you? Good. You're very gifted, Pierre, gifted with money, breeding, intelligence, and a very pretty face. I taught you all I could about being a gentleman. The war has taught you about the perfidies and cruelties of mankind. Now, Quennel Quinton has taught you never to accept anything at face value, even if it is personally painful for you to delve into a subject. He has also taught you a measure of humility, hasn't he, showing you that, for all your grand intelligence, you can still be duped. All round, I'd say the thing was a particularly satisfactory exercise.''

"I exist only to please you, Father,'' Pierre drawled sarcastically.

"Of course you do," André acknowledged in complete seriousness. "Never forget it. The only obstacle to becoming a complete gentleman left before you now is for you to accomplish some good, unselfish work—some compassionate assistance to one of the helpless wretches of mankind. You have made a good start by helping your friend Sherbourne secure the affections of Quinton's supposed daughter, Victoria, but as you were trying to rid yourself of the title of murder suspect at the time, I cannot feel that your actions were completely altruistic. Yes, I would like to see you perform some good deed, with not a single thought of personal reward. Do you think you can handle that on your own, or shall I devise some scheme to set you on your way?"

Pierre stared at his father unblinkingly. "There are times when I actually believe I could hate you, Father," he said, unable to hide a wry smile.

"Yes, of course," Andé replied silkily. "Truthfully, I believe I should be disappointed in you if you were to fall on my neck, thanking me. Shall we go in to dinner?"

Chapter Two

Pierre lingered in the country with André for another two days, the two men rebuilding their former good relationship on a sounder, more solid base before the younger Standish reluctantly took his leave, his father's admonition—to find himself a humanizing good deed as soon as may be for the sake of his immortal soul—following after him as his coachman sprung the horses.

"A good deed," Pierre repeated, settling himself against the midnight-blue velvet squabs of the traveling coach that was the envy of London. "What do you think of that, Duvall, my friend?"

The manservant gave a Gallic shrug, shaking his head. *"Il vous rit au nez."*

"Father doesn't laugh in my *nose*, Duvall; he laughs in my face, and no, I don't think so. Not this time," Pierre corrected, smiling at the French interpretation of the old saying. "This time I think he is deadly serious, more's the pity. My dearest, most loving father thinks I need to—"

"Tomber à plat ventre," Duvall intoned gravely, folding his scrawny arms across his thin chest.

"Not really. You French may fall flat on your stomachs, Duvall. We English much prefer to land on our faces, if indeed we must take the fall at all. And how will you ever develop a workable knowledge of English if you insist upon lapsing into French the moment we are alone? Consider yourself forbidden the language from this moment, if you please."

"Your father, he wishes for you to fall flat on your face," Duvall recited obediently, then sighed deeply, so that his employer should be aware that he had injured him most gravely.

"Bless you, Duvall. Now, to get back to the point. I have been acting the fool these past years, a fact I will acknowledge only to you, and only this one time. There's nothing else for it—I must seek out a good deed and perform it with humble dedication and no thought for my own interests. Do you suppose the opportunity for good deeds lies thick on the ground in Mayfair? No, I imagine not. Ah, well, one can only strive to do one's best."

"Humph!" was the manservant's only reply before he turned his head to one side and ordered himself to go to sleep in the hope that the soft, well-sprung swaying of the traveling coach would not then turn his delicate Gallic stomach topsy-turvy.

Standish marveled silently yet again at the endless effrontery of his employee. The man, unlike the remainder of Pierre's acquaintances, had no fear of him—and precious little awe. It was refreshing, this lack of deference, which was why Pierre treasured the spritely little Frenchman, who had been displaced to Piccadilly during Napoleon's rush to conquer all the known world. Reaching across to lay a light blanket over the man's shoulders, for it was September and the morning was cool, Pierre sat back once more, determined to enjoy the passing scenery.

It was shortly after regaining the main roadway, following a leisurely lunch at the busy Rose and Cross Inn—Pierre being particularly fond of country-cured ham—that it happened. One of the two burly outriders accompanying the coach called out to the driver to stop at once, for there was something moving in the small mountain of baggage strapped in the boot of the coach.

"How wonderfully intriguing. Do you suppose it is an animal of some sort?" Pierre asked the two outriders, the coachman, and a slightly green-looking Duvall a minute later as the small group assembled behind the halted coach. He lightly prodded the canvas wrapping with the tip of his cane, just at the spot the outrider had indicated. "I do pray it is not a fox, for I will confess that I am not a devotee

13

of blood sports. Oh, dear. It moved again just then, didn't it? My curiosity knows no bounds, I must tell you.''

"It's a blinkin' stowaway, that's wot it tis,'' decided the second outrider, just home from an extended absence at sea, a trip prompted not by his desire to explore the world, but rather at the expressed insistence of a press gang that had tapped him on the noggin with a heavy club and tossed him aboard a merchantman bound for India. "Let's yank 'im out an' keelhaul 'im!''

Pierre turned to look at the man, a large, beefy fellow whose hamlike hands were already closed into tight fists. "So violent, my friend? Why don't we just boil the poor soul in oil and have done with it?''

Raising his voice slightly, Pierre went on, ''You there— in the boot—I suggest you join us out here on the road, if you please. You can't be too comfortable in there, knowing the amount of baggage I deem necessary for travel through the wilds of Sussex. When did you decide to join us? Perhaps when my baggage was undone to unearth my personal linens and utensils back at the so lovely Rose and Whatever Inn? Come out now, we shan't hurt you.''

"Oi can't,'' a high, whiny voice complained from beneath the canvas. ''Yer gots me trussed up like a blinkin' goose in 'ere!''

Pierre tipped his head to one side, inspecting the canvas-covered boot. ''Our unexpected passenger has a point there, gentlemen. It really was too bad of you, wasn't it, even as I applaud your obvious high regard for the welfare of my personal possessions. Perhaps one of you will be so good as to lend some assistance to our beleaguered stowaway before he causes himself an injury?''

Less than a minute later the canvas had been drawn away to reveal a very small, very dirty face. ''Hello. What have we here?'' Pierre asked, peering into the semidarkness of the boot.

"Yer gots Jeremy 'Olloway, that wot yer gots!'' the young boy shot back defiantly, pushing out his lower lip to blow a long strand of greasy blond hair from his eyes.

"Now, stands back whilst Oi boosts m'self outta this blinkin' 'ellhole!"

"How lovely," Pierre drawled. "Such elegant speech. And a good day to you too, Master Holloway. Obviously, my friends, we have discovered a runaway young peer, bent on a lark in the country. Gentlemen, let us make our bows to Master Holloway."

"That's no gentry mort," the burly outrider corrected, narrowly eyeing the young boy as he climbed down from his hiding place, and quickly clamping a heavy hand on Jeremy's thin shoulder as the lad looked ready to bolt for the concealment of the trees on the side of the road. "This 'ere ain't nothin' but a bleedin' sweep!"

"Oi'm not!" Jeremy shot back, sticking out his chin, as if his denial could erase the damning evidence of his torn, sooty shirt and the scraped, burned-covered arms and legs that stuck out awkwardly from beneath his equally ragged, too-small suit of clothes.

"Of course you're not a sweep," Pierre agreed silkily, suppressing the need to touch his scented lace handkerchief to his nostrils as he looked at Jeremy and saw a quick solution to his need to do a good deed. "But if you *were* a sweep, and running away from an evil master who abused you most abominably, I should think I could find it in my heart to take you up with us for a space, until, say, we reach London? Listening to your speech, and detecting a rightful disdain for those so troublesome 'aitches', I believe you might feel at home in Piccadilly?"

Jeremy, who had begun eyeing Pierre assessingly, positively blossomed at the mention of Piccadilly. Quickly suppressing his excitement, he scuffed one bare big toe in the dirt and remarked coolly: "If Oi *wuz* a sweep—which Oi'm not, o'course—Oi might wants ter take yer up on that, guv'nor. The Piccadilly thing, yer knows."

Duvall immediately burst into a rapid stream of emotional French, wringing his hands as he alternately cursed and pleaded with his master to reconsider this folly. Better they should all bed down with *une mouffette,* a skunk! Oh, woe, oh, woe! Poor master, to have a cracked bell in his head. Poor Duvall, to be so overset that he could not even think which saint to pray to!

Jeremy stood stoically by, grimy paws jammed down hard on even grimier hips, waiting for the barrage of French to run itself down, then said, "Aw, dub yer mummer, froggie. Oi ain't 'eared such a ruckus since ol' 'awkins burnt 'isself wit 'is own poker!"

Duvall stopped in mid-exclamation to glare down at the boy, his lips pursed, his eyes bulging. *"Mon Dieu!"* he declared. "This insect, this crawling bug, he has called me a frog. I will not stand firm for such an insult!"

"Stand still," Pierre corrected smoothly, at last succumbing to the need to filter his breathing air through the handkerchief. "Now, if the histrionics are behind us—and I most sincerely pray that they are—I suggest that Jeremy crawl back into the boot, sans the cover, and the rest of us also return to our proper places. I wish to make London before Father Christmas."

Satisfied that he was doing his good deed just as his father had recommended—and rescuing Jeremy from an evil master certainly seemed to qualify—Pierre once more settled himself against the midnight-blue velvet squabs and began mentally preparing a missive to his father detailing his charitable wonderfulness. "And that will be the end of that," he said aloud, eyeing Duvall levelly and daring the manservant to contradict him.

The coach had gone no more than a mile when it stopped once more, the coachman hauling on the reins so furiously that Pierre found himself clutching the handstrap for fear of tumbling onto the narrow width of flooring between the seats.

"I am a reasonably good man, a loving son," he assured himself calmly as he reached to open the small door that would allow him to converse with the driver. "I have my faults, I suppose, but I have never been a purposely *mean* person. Why then, Duvall, do you suppose I feel this overwhelming desire to draw and quarter my coachman?"

"If there truly is a God, the dirty little person will have been flung to the road on his dripping nose," Duvall grumbled by way of an answer, adjusting his jacket after picking himself up from the floor of the coach where, as his reflexes were not so swift as his employer's, the driver's abrupt stop had landed him.

"Driver?" Pierre inquired urbanely, holding open the small door. "May I assume you have an explanation, or have you merely decided it is time you took yourself into the bushes to answer nature's call?"

"Sorry, sir," the coachman mumbled apologetically, leaning down to peer into the darkened interior of the coach. "But you see, sir, there's a lady in the road. At least, I think it's a lady."

Pierre's left brow lifted fractionally. "A lady," he repeated consideringly. "How prudent of you not to run her down. My compliments on both your driving and your charity, although I cannot but wonder at your difficulty in deciding the gender of our roadblock. Perhaps now you might take it upon yourself to ask this lady to move?"

"I can't, sir," the coachman responded, the slight quiver in his voice reflecting both his lingering shock at avoiding a calamity and his fearful respect of his employer. "Like I told yer—she's in the road. It's a lady for sure, 'cause I can see her feet. I think mayhap she's dead, and can't move."

Pierre's lips twitched as he remarked quietly, "Her feet? An odd way to determine gender, Duvall, wouldn't you say?" His next communication to the coachman followed, both his words and his offhand tone announcing that he was decidedly unimpressed. "Dead, you say, coachman? That *would* be an impediment to movement, wouldn't it?"

Duvall quickly blessed himself, muttering something in French that may have been "Blessed Mary protect us, and why couldn't it have been the sweep?"

"A dead lady in the middle of the road," Pierre mused again out loud, already moving toward the coach door. "I imagine I should see this deceased lady for myself." With one foot in the road, he paused to order quietly: "Arm yourself, coachman, and instruct the outriders to scan the trees for horsemen. This may be a trap. There are still robbers along this roadway.

"Although I would have thought it would be easier to throw a dead tree into the road, rather than a dead lady," he added under his breath as he disengaged Duvall's convulsive grip on his coattail. "Please, my good friend," he admonished with a smile. "Consider the fabric, if not your long hours with the iron."

Pierre stepped completely onto the roadway, nodding almost imperceptibly to the two outriders while noting with mingled comfort and amusement that the coachman was now brandishing a very mean-looking blunderbuss at the ready. A quick look to the rear of the coach assured him that his Good Deed was still firmly anchored in the boot, as the streetwise Jeremy Holloway's dirt-streaked face was peeping around the edge of the coach, his eyes wide as saucers. "Oi've got yer back, guv'nor," the boy whispered hoarsely. "Don't yer go worryin' 'bout dat."

"Such loyalty deserves a reward," Pierre whispered back at the boy. "If we get out of this with our skin intact, Master Holloway, I shall allow you to sit up top with the coachman." As the coachman gave out with an audible groan, Pierre began strolling toward the standing horses, his demeanor decidedly casual, as if he were merely taking the air in the park.

Once he had come up beside the off-leader, he could see the woman, who was, just as the coachman had reported, lying facedown in the roadway and looking, for all intents and purposes, extremely dead. She was dressed in a man's drab grey cloak, its hood having fallen forward to hide her face as well as whatever gown she wore beneath its voluminous expanse. Her stockinged, shoeless feet—small feet attached to rather shapely slim ankles, he noted automatically, for he was a man who appreciated female beauty—extended from beneath the hem of the cloak, but her hands were pinned beneath her, out of sight.

He walked to within two paces of her, then used the tip of his cane to lightly nudge her in the rib cage. There was no response, either from the woman or from the heavily wooded perimeters of the road. If the woman was only feigning injury and in league with highwaymen, her compatriots were taking their sweet time in making their presence known.

Gingerly lowering himself onto his haunches, and being most careful not to muddy the knees of his skin-tight fawn buckskin breeches, Pierre took hold of the woman in the area of her shoulder and gently turned her onto her back.

"Ohh." The sound was soft, barely more than a faint expulsion of air, but it had come from the woman. Obviously she had not yet expired, not that her life expectancy could be numbered in more than a few minutes or hours if she were to continue to lie in the middle of the roadway.

"She toes-cocked, guv'nor, or wot?"

Jeremy's voice, coming from somewhere behind Pierre's left shoulder, made him realize that he had been paying attention to the woman when he should have been listening for highwaymen. "She's not dead, if that's what that colorful expression is meant to imply," he supplied tonelessly, pushing the hood from the woman's face so that he could get a better look at her.

What he saw made him inhale involuntarily, his left brow raising a fraction in surprise. The woman was little more than a girl, and she was exceedingly beautiful, in an ethereal way. Masses of softly waving hair the color of midnight tangled across her ashen, dirt-smeared face, trailing strands that lovingly clung to the small, finely sculpted features that carried the unmistakable stamp of good bloodlines.

Quickly seeking out her limp arm to feel for her pulse, Pierre mentally noted the fragile slimness of her wrist and the slender perfection of her hand and fingers. Her *cold* hand and *frigid* fingers.

"Master Holloway, be a good boy and go tell Duvall to bring me a blanket," Pierre ordered without looking away from the young woman's face, wrapping her once more in the worn grey cloak. "And have him bring my flask as well. This poor child is chilled through to the bone."

Once Duvall had brought the blanket, Pierre draped it

over the young woman and hefted her upper body onto his knees, intent on forcing her to drink some of the warming brandy. It was no use. The brandy ran into her mouth, only to dribble back onto her chin. Handing the flask back to his manservant—who immediately took a restorative dose of the fiery liquid for himself—Pierre lifted the young woman completely into his arms and returned to the coach.

"Yer takin' 'er with us?" the seafaring outrider questioned worriedly. "Wimmen is bad luck aboard, that's wot they are. Always wuz, always will be. Better yer toss 'er back. She's a small one anyways."

Pierre silenced the man with a look. "Turn this equipage about at once, if you please. I have a sudden desire to return to Standish Court. And don't spare the horses," he ordered the driver as he swept into the coach, the young woman lolling bonelessly in his arms.

Beneath his breath he added, "I do begin to believe my loving parent has put a fatherly curse on me. I am suddenly overrun with unlooked-for Good Deeds. But, being a loving son, and not a greedy man, I also believe that at least one of these humanizing projects rightfully belongs to him. Duvall," he called out, "tell the coachman that Jeremy is to ride atop with him."

Chapter Three

"Coo, guv'nor, would yer jist look at dat! Dat gentry mort looks jist like yer—wit a coffin o' snow plopped on 'is 'ead!"

André Standish leveled a cool, assessing look at the untidy urchin perched on top of the traveling coach, then descended the few remaining steps to the gravel drive and addressed his son through the lowered coach window. "An acquaintance of yours, Pierre? He has an interesting way with description. Have you lost your way and must retrace your steps, or have you somehow learned that cook is preparing your favorite meal for tonight—a lovely brown ragôut of lamb with peas—and it is your stomach that brings you back to me?"

"My current favorite meal is rare roasted beef with horseradish sauce," Pierre corrected, "although I know it is rude of me to point out this single lapse in your seemingly faultless store of information about me. And no," he said, shifting the human weight in his arms in preparation for leaving the coach, "much as I love you, I have not lost my way. May I infringe upon your affection by prevailing upon you to open this door?"

André complied with a courtly bow, flinging open the door and personally letting down the steps. A moment later, Pierre was standing beside him in the drive, the young woman still lying limply in his arms.

The older Standish gently pushed back the hood of the grey cloak, revealing the young woman's face. "I detect the smell of brandy. I foolishly thought I had raised you better than this. Surely you haven't taken to drugging your females, Pierre?''

''Not lately, Father. My coachman nearly ran over her as she lay in the road.''

''Unconscious? A head injury?'' André asked, not wasting time in useless questions as to how the female had come to be in the road in the first place.

''Most definitely unconscious.''

''Have you learned her name?'' André asked as the two men hurriedly mounted the steps to the house, Jeremy Holloway at their heels until Duvall stuck out one foot and tripped him so that he landed facedown in the drive.

''I like to think of her as Miss Penance,'' Pierre replied immediately. ''Whether she is mine or yours remains to be seen. Duvall,'' he called over his shoulder, ''I saw that. For shame. I would not have believed it of you. Now wash it and feed it and put it to bed.''

Duvall, having no trouble in understanding who ''it'' was, tottered over to lean against the side of the traveling coach and buried his head in his hands.

''She's still sleeping?'' André asked the question three hours later as Pierre entered the drawing room, having excused himself after dinner to check on their patient.

''Hartley assures me that she'll sleep through to the morning,'' he told his father. ''It may only be a butler's opinion, but as the doctor said much the same thing before he left, I believe we can safely assume it's true. She's got a lump the size of a pigeon's egg on the side of her head.''

''Poor Miss Penance,'' André commented, accepting the snifter of brandy his son offered him. ''She'll have a bruiser of a headache when she wakes, I fear. Now, do you think it's possible for you to tell me about the urchin? We somehow neglected to speak of him over dinner, perhaps hoping to preserve our appetites, for he was most unappealing when last I saw him. Duvall appears to dislike him, a lack of affection that seems to be mutual. I happened to pass by the bedroom as your man was giving the boy a bath, you see. The language spewing forth from the pair of them was enough to put me to the blush.''

Pierre took a sip of brandy. ''Duvall likes everyone very little, save me, of course, for whom he would gladly die if asked. A man could become quite full of himself, knowing that. But to answer your question, young Master Jeremy Holloway is a runaway—having escaped the life of a chimney sweep, if my powers of deduction are correct. He chose my coach as his route to freedom when we stopped for luncheon.''

''An enterprising young lad,'' André remarked, watching the burnished liquid swirl and gleam as he rubbed the brandy snifter lightly back and forth between his palms. ''Oh, by the by—young Master Holloway would like to have a hot poker inserted in an area of Duvall's anatomy that is not usually spoken of in more polite circles. Duvall, in his turn, would like the boy deposited in a dirty sack posthaste and drowned in the goldfish pond—as I am convinced my understanding of gutter French is still reasonably accurate. My goodness, I begin to feel like a spy reporting to his superior.''

''Duvall likes to think of himself as bloodthirsty,'' Pierre remarked calmly. ''Even taking Duvall's sensibilities into account, however,'' he went on silkily, ''I do believe I shall take Jeremy as my Good Deed, and leave the disposition of Miss Penance to you.''

André blinked once. ''Indeed,'' he drawled, setting the snifter down very carefully. ''And might I ask why I'm to be gifted with an unknown female with a lump the size of a pigeon's egg on her pate?''

''Of course.'' Pierre lifted his own snifter and tipped it slightly in André's direction. ''I won't even remind you of how you maneuvered me so meanly once you learned about Quinton. Shall we drink to *poetic justice*, Father?''

The morning arrived very early, very abruptly, and in full voice.

''How dare you! Get your hands off me! At once! Do you hear me?''

Obviously the injured young lady had come to her senses with a vengeance. Mere seconds after her screams had stopped, Pierre—who had been sleeping most peacefully in the adjoining chamber—skidded to a halt just inside the bedroom that had been assigned to Miss Penance, still tying the sash of his maroon banyan around his trim waist.

"I imagine you can be heard in Bond Street, brat," he commented, running his fingers through his sleep-mussed hair and ruefully looking down at his bare legs and feet. Raising his head, he addressed the butler, whom he espied backing toward the door to the hall, a china cup and saucer nervously chattering against the silver tray he was clutching with two hands, his face white with shock. "Ah, Hartley, dear fellow, what seems to be the matter?"

Hartley's lips moved, quivered actually, but no words came forth.

"What seems to be the problem?" the woman asked. "What seems to be the problem! I awoke to see this *man* leaning over my bed! *That's* the problem! And why are you asking him? And who are you? You're not even dressed, for pity's sake. What has the world come to when a lady can't get some sleep without all the world creeping into her bedchamber, with only the good Lord knows what on their minds, that's what I want to know. Well, don't just stand there with your mouths at half cock. You both have some explaining to do!"

"Hartley, you may retire now," Pierre offered kindly as the elderly butler looked about to expire from mingled shock and indignation. "And please accept my congratulations. I didn't know you were still considered to be such a danger to the ladies."

Leaning his shoulder against the doorjamb, his arms folded against his chest, one bare leg crossed negligently over the other at the ankles, Pierre then allowed his gaze to take a slow, leisurely assessment of the young woman occupying the bed.

She was still as beautiful as his initial impression of her had indicated, with her small features lovingly framed by a heavy mass of coal-black hair, her pale skin made creamy where her slim throat rose above the fine white lawn of Eleanore Standish's nightgown. His first sight of her long-lashed, blue-violet eyes only reconfirmed his opinion. However, she might not be quite as young as he had first thought, for the light of intelligence burned brightly in her eyes. "Unless it's fever," he hedged aloud, knowing his wits weren't usually at their sharpest this early in the day. His early morning wits or the lack of them to one side for the moment, Miss Penance was still a most remarkably beautiful young woman.

"Well?" she asked, pushing her hands straight out in front of her, palms upward and gesturing toward him. "Have you somehow been turned to marble, sir? Perhaps I should remind you of your current situation? You're in a lady's bedchamber without invitation. I suggest you retire before I'm forced to do you an injury."

Pierre smiled. "Oh, Father's going to adore you," he said silkily. "What's your name, little Amazon? We can't go on calling you Miss Penance, although my spur of the moment christening now seems to border on the inspired. Please, madam, give me a name."

"My name?" she croaked, wincing.

"Your name," Pierre repeated. "As you're sleeping in my father's house, I don't believe it is an out-of-the-way demand."

Miss Penance slumped against the pillows, suddenly appearing to be even smaller than she had before, her chin on her chest. "So you don't know who I am either," she said in a small voice, all her bravado deserting her. "I had hoped—"

She sniffed, a portion of her spunk reasserting itself. "I should have known I'd be looking for mare's nests, asking for some spark of intelligence from a man who has that much hair on his legs and is vain enough to consider showing it off to strangers."

"Eight to five you're a parson's eldest," Pierre was stung into replying. "And a Methodist parson to boot. Only the worse sort of strumpet or a holier-than-thou old maid would even dare utter the word "leg" in front of a

25

gentleman. Somehow, I can't quite picture you in the role of strumpet. You dislike men entirely too much. Which leaves us with only the other alternative. Now, are you really trying to tell me that you have no recollection of your own name?''

"Don't be ridiculous! Of course I know my own name! Everyone knows his own name,'' she shot back at him. "I just—'' Her voice began to lose some of its confidence. "I just seem to have, um, momentarily *misplaced* the memory. It'll come to me any time now. I'm sure of it.''

"How reassuring,'' Pierre soothed, slowly advancing into the room. "And, of course, once you succeed in locating this truant name, you'll doubtless inform me as to why you were lying unconscious in the middle of the roadway just north of here, obstructing traffic and upsetting my coachman no end. It's the merest bagatelle—no more than a trifling inconvenience—this temporary lapse.''

The violet eyes shot blue-purple flame. "Oh, do be quiet, Mr.—''

"Standish,'' Pierre supplied immediately, lowering himself into a seated position on the bottom of the bed. "Pierre Standish. See how easy that was. Now you try it. How utterly charmed I am to meet you, Miss—''

She nodded her head three times, as if the movement would jog her memory. "Miss . . . Miss . . . oh, drat! I don't know! *I don't know!*''

"Quietly, my dear Miss Forgetful, quietly,'' Pierre scolded absently. "We shall abandon this exercise momentarily, as it seems only to annoy you, and speak of other things. How is your head? You sustained a rather nasty bump on it, one way or another.''

She reached up to gingerly inspect the lump she had discovered earlier upon awakening. "It's still there, if that's any answer,'' she told him. "Your guess is as good as mine as to how I came to have it. And, even though I am sure it matters little to you, it hurts like the very devil.''

Pierre frowned at her use of the word "devil.'' Tipping his head to one side, he commented, "I believe we can dispense with the notion that you are a parson's daughter. Your language is too broad."

"Then I am to be the worst sort of strumpet?" she asked, narrowing her eyes belligerently. "Thank you. Thank you very much."

Pierre shook his head, "No, not a strumpet, either. You're much too insulting. You'd have starved by now."

"Perhaps I am a thief," she suggested, pulling the blankets more firmly under her chin. "Perhaps you should be locking up your family silver at this very moment, for fear I shall lope off with it the instant I find my clothes. I may assume that I have some clothing somewhere? Not that I'm likely to recognize it any more than I recognize this nightgown I have on now."

"There's no reason for you to recognize it. It was my mother's," Pierre told her. "She died several years ago."

"I'm surprised."

"Surprised that my mother is deceased?" Pierre questioned, looking at her oddly.

"Surprised that she lived so long, with you for a son," she answered meanly, for even a fool could see that she was feeling very mean.

"*Touché*, madam. I believe that evens up our insults quite nicely." Pierre rose from the bed and turned from her before he spoke again. "I'll send a maid with some breakfast," he said just as he reached the doorway to his own bedchamber. "That is, if I recover from the wounds your tongue has inflicted. Later, when you are more rested, my father will doubtless wish to interview you. Pray don't repeat your latest attempt at nastiness to him, for he loved my mother very much."

"I'm sorry," she called after him. "Really, I'm sorry. I shouldn't have said that. It's just . . . it's just that I'm really very upset. I mean, I don't even know where I am, let alone who I am. Please—forgive me."

Pierre turned to look at the young woman now sitting up in the bed, her violet eyes drenched with tears. "Neither of us has been very nice, have we?" he said. "It happens that way with some people, I've heard. We have already decided not to like each other, no matter how little Dame Reason is involved in the decision. Let us agree to forgive each other, madam, and have done with it.''

"Agreed!" she said smiling for the first time, the unexpected beauty of it making a direct hit on Pierre's senses, so that he blinked twice, said nothing, and left the room, suddenly uncomfortable at being dressed in nothing more than his banyan.

A hot bath helped to ease the soreness she had felt over every inch of her body from the moment she had first awakened in the beautiful, sunlit bedchamber.

The young maid who had introduced herself as Susan had carefully washed her hair, massaging away some of her tension and banishing the headache that had been pounding against her temples.

The meal of poached eggs, country bacon, toast, and tea had erased the gnawing hunger that had made her believe her stomach must have been worrying that her throat had somehow been cut.

But nothing could ease the terrible, blood-chilling panic that shivered through her body each time she attempted to remember who she was, or where she lived, or how she had come to be lying unconscious in the middle of a roadway.

"I just don't remember!" she said out loud as she sat at the dressing table in the nightgown and robe Susan had brought her after her bath, glaring at her unfamiliar reflection, her chin in her hands. "I don't remember anything; nothing before waking up here this morning."

"There are many who would not curse such a lapse, but rather rejoice in it. Good afternoon, Miss Penance. I'm André Standish, your host. Forgive me, but I did knock."

"You—you look just like him," she was stung into saying as she stared into the mirror, where André's reflection smiled back at her. "If it weren't for the color of your hair, I'd swear—"

"Ah, you'd swear," André interrupted. "I see my son has not exaggerated. You are an enigma, aren't you, Miss

28

Penance? You have the look and accent of a lady, but your conversation is sprinkled with words most well-brought-up young females have been taught to shun. Of course, there was a time, more years ago than I care to recall, when all the best ladies were shockingly frank in their speech, but that time has since passed, more's the pity. Perhaps you were raised solely by your father, or a doting uncle. That would explain it, wouldn't it?"

She sat quite still, listening to the sound of his voice more than his actual words. His tone was so gentle, so reassuring. "No," she answered, suddenly sleepy, and wondering why she felt she could lean her head against his arm and doze, secure in the knowledge that he'd never hurt her. "No, I don't think so. Men seem to frighten me—except you, that is. I was very afraid of your son this morning. I don't think I've been around men very much."

"Pierre can be most formidable, even in his banyan. *Especially* in his banyan, I imagine." André laid a hand on her shoulder. "You're frightened, and with every right. Forgive me for trying to prod you into memory. There's no rush, you know. We shall take this thing one day at a time. Now, come lie down on the bed for a while. You must be exhausted. I've already sent for the doctor, but he is busy with someone who is really ill and not merely confused by a bump on the head. He sent along a note assuring me that you'll remember everything in time. He will be here tomorrow to answer any questions you might have."

She allowed herself to be helped into bed. Looking up at André, she said, "You're not at all like your son after all. You're very nice."

"Pierre's a beast, I'm ashamed to say. Quite uncivilized," André confessed with a smile and a slight shake of his silver head. "Were I you, I should stay as far removed from him as possible. Now, get some rest while I go downstairs and cudgel my brain into coming up with a female companion for you. It isn't correct for you to be the lone young woman in a masculine household."

29

She was very sleepy, but she didn't miss the meaning of his words. "Then—then you think I'm a young lady?"

"Was there every any doubt?" André replied, winking at her as he closed the door behind him.

Chapter Four

The young lady Pierre had dubbed Miss Penance walked aimlessly along the twisting gravel paths of the substantial Standish Court ornamental gardens, idly swinging a yellow chip straw bonnet by its pink satin ribbons, her feet dragging only a little in the soft, too-large kid slippers that had once belonged to Eleanore Standish.

The gardens were glorious, a fairyland of flowers and evergreens and whimsical statuary, all bathed in the warmth of a sunny late summer's afternoon. It was a perfect place to spend a few quiet moments, which was the reason André Standish had suggested it to her earlier, after she had risen from her nap.

So far, neither her nap, the walk, nor the peacefulness of her surroundings had jogged her memory. She had been without it for only a few hours, but she measured its loss minute by minute, and the gravity and scope of that loss were gnawing at her, causing the still tender bump on her head to throb most painfully.

She could be anybody—or nobody. It would be awful to be a Nobody. No one would send out an alarm for a Nobody. A Nobody could disappear from the face of the earth without a trace and no one would care, no one would feel the loss. A Somebody would be missed, and an immediate search would be instituted. Besides, she didn't feel like a Nobody; she felt like a Somebody.

"That's no great help," she told herself out loud. "Everybody wants to be a Somebody. Now, how do you suppose I know that?"

Her seemingly selective memory was what really upset

and confused her. How could she know so much and still not know who she was? She knew the name of that flower climbing the trellis over there—it was a morning glory, a purple one.

She knew she was in Sussex, for Susan had told her. She knew Sussex was in England, and that Susan had not told her. She knew where Austria was, and could name at least three principal crops of France. She knew the Italian word for head was *capo*, but did not know how she knew it.

She was sure she had always particularly favored chicken as it had been presented to her for luncheon in her room, and could name the ingredients used in its preparation. She had counted to three thousand as she had sat in her bath, and probably could have continued to count for the remainder of the day without problem.

So why couldn't she remember her name?

She could be married, for pity's sake! That thought stopped her short, and she bit her lip in trepidation. She could have a husband somewhere. Children. Crying for her, missing her. No, she didn't feel married. Could a person feel married? How did being unmarried feel?

She could be a bad person. Why, she could be a thief, as she had suggested to Pierre Standish. Perhaps she had been discovered with her hand in some good wife's silver drawer, and had been running from the constable when she had fallen, hitting her head on a stone.

She could be a murderess! She could have murdered a man—her husband, perhaps?—and been fleeing the scene of that dastardly crime in the dead man's cloak when she had somehow come to grief in the middle of the roadway.

Pierre Standish had certainly been unflattering when he pointed out that her speech, although cultured in accent, contained a few expressions that were not normally considered to be ladylike. Ladies did not rob or murder.

The thought of Pierre Standish had her moving again, as if she could distance herself from thinking of the man. How dare he enter her bedchamber in such a state of indecent undress! And once he had realized what he had done, why hadn't he excused himself and retired, as any reasonable man would have done, rather than plunk himself down on the bottom of her bed so familiarly and immediately commence insulting her? He hadn't had an ounce of pity for her plight. As a matter of fact, he seemed to find the entire situation vaguely amusing. No wonder her language had not been the best.

No, she didn't know much, but she knew she didn't like Pierre Standish.

She did like André Standish, however. The older Standish was kindness itself, fatherly, and certainly sympathetic to her plight. After all, hadn't he told her not to worry, that his hospitality was hers until she rediscovered her identity, and even beyond, if that discovery proved to present new problems for her? Hadn't he assigned Susan as her personal maid, and even promised to provide a female chaperone as soon as may be? Hadn't he even gifted her with the use of his late wife's entire wardrobe?

The gown she was wearing now was six years out of fashion and marred by the helpful but vaguely inept alterations Susan had performed on the bodice, waist, and hem as her new mistress napped, but it was still a most beautiful creation of sprigged muslin and cotton lace.

She smoothed the skirt of the gown with her hands, grateful once again for being able to wear it, and then purposely made her mind go blank, concentrating on nothing as she continued to walk, not knowing that her appearance was more than passably pleasing, it was beautiful.

Her hair, that unbelievably thick and lengthy mane of softly waving ebony, was tucked into a huge topknot, with several errant curling tendrils clinging to her forehead, cheeks, and nape.

Her face was flawless, except for a lingering paleness and a vaguely cloudy look to her unusual violet eyes. Her mouth, generous and wide, drooped imperceptibly at the corners as she stopped in front of a rose bush, picked a large red bloom, and began methodically stripping away its petals, tossing them over the bush.

She looked young, innocent, vulnerable, and just a little sad.

" 'Ey! Gets yourself somewheres else, fer criminy's sake! Yer wants ter blow m'lay?"

She turned her head this way and that, trying to figure out where the voice was coming from.

"Oi says, take yerself off, yer ninny. Find yerself yer own 'idey-'ole."

"Hidey-hole?" she repeated, leaning forward a little, as she was sure that voice had come from behind the rose bush. "Who or what are you hiding from?"

"The froggie, o'course. Who else do yer think? Now, take yerself off!"

She wasn't afraid, for the voice sounded very young and more than a little frightened. Her smooth brow furrowed in confusion at his words, though, and she asked, "Hiding from a frog, are you? Well, if that isn't above everything silly! I would imagine you'd be more likely to come upon a frog in the gardens, wouldn't you? If you don't wish to come face to face with one, don't you think it would be preferable to hide where frogs don't go?"

Jeremy Holloway was so overcome by this blatant idiocy that he forgot himself and stood up, just to get a good look at the woman who could spout anything so ridiculous. "Yer dicked in the nob, lady?" he exclaimed in consternation, then quickly ducked again, whining, "Yer seen me now. Yer gonna cry beef on me?"

She leaned forward some more and was able to see a boy as he crouched on all fours, ready to scurry off to find a new hidey-hole. "If you mean, am I going to turn you in, no, I don't think I am. After all, who would I turn you in to in the first place?"

"Dat froggie, dat's who! And all because Oi gots a few active citizens. Oi asks yer—is dat fair? Show me a lily white wot's ain't gots some, dat's wot Oi says."

Her head was reeling. "Are you speaking English?" she questioned, careful not to move for fear the boy would run off before she could get a good look at him.

All was quiet for a few moments, but at last, his decision made, Jeremy poked his head above the rose bush, looked furtively right and left, and then abandoned his hiding place. "Yer the one m' gingerbread man found in the road yesterdee," he told her unnecessarily. *"Yer* cleaned up right well, Oi suppose. But not this cove. Not Jeremy 'Olloway. Nobody's gonna dunk this cove in Adam's ale agin."

"Thank you, I think," she answered, beating down the urge to step back a pace or two, for, in truth, Jeremy didn't smell too fresh. The boy was filthy, his clothing ragged and three sizes too small. "You might too. I imagine Adam's ale is water? What's a lily white, Jeremy, and whose citizens are active? And a gingerbread man?"

With an expression on his thin face that suggested she must be the most ignorant person ever to walk the earth, Jeremy supplied impatiently, "A lily white's a sweep, o' course. Everyun knows dat. Oi'm really a 'prentice, or Oi wuz, till yesterdee. My mum sold me ter ol' 'Awkins fer 'alf a crown, which is more than m' brother went fer. Wot else? Oh, yer. A gingerbread man is a rich gentry cove, like Mr. Standish. 'Appy now? Yer asks more questions than a parson."

"Lily white because they're so very dirty? Oh, that's very good," she commented, smiling at Jeremy, her heart wrung by his offhanded reference to what must have been a terrible experience. "But what's an active citizen?"

Jeremy put his head down, scuffing one bare foot against the gravel path. "Lice," he mumbled, then raised his head to fairly shout: "An' 'e ain't stickin' Jeremy 'Olloway's 'air in no tar an' shavin' it! Oi'll skewer 'im first—an' so Oi told 'im, jist afore Oi kicked 'im an' loped off! 'E didn't foller me, 'cause 'e 'ates the ground Oi dirties an' wants me gone. 'E told me so 'imself."

"Mon Dieu! There you are, you *vilain moineau,* you nasty sparrow! Please to grab his ear, mademoiselle, so that I might cage him! I have the water hot, and the scissors is at the ready!"

More rapidly than she could react, the scene exploded before her eyes. A thin, harried-looking Frenchman appeared in front of her, a stout rope in one hand, a large empty sack in the other, and Jeremy Holloway disappeared, faster than a gold piece vanishes into a beggar's pocket.

"You have let for him to escape me again!" the Frenchman accused, his watery eyes narrowed as he glared at her.

"You frightened him, the poor boy," she accused, feeling protective.

"Please not to put in your grain of salt, mademoiselle," he returned nastily, drawing himself up to his full height. "I have been run to the rags searching for the small monster. I have been made sore with trying."

She understood. In that moment she understood something else as well—Jeremy's words coming back to her—and the light of battle entered her eyes. "Oh, do be quiet, *froggie*," she ordered, privately pleased with herself.

"Froggie!" The servant's head snapped back with the insult, as if he had been slapped.

They stood there, the pair of them frozen in their aggressive stances for several seconds, then Duvall opened his mouth to speak. Fortunately for his opponent, something else took his attention just as he was about to begin, for his response to her name-calling was sure to be terrible, if unintelligible to anyone not familiar with gutter French.

"I say, Duvall, must I do everything for you?" asked a weary voice from somewhere behind them, and both of them turned to see Pierre Standish coming down the pathway, Jeremy Holloway's left earlobe firmly pinched between his thumb and forefinger. "I set you a simple chore, and now, more than four and twenty hours later, the evidence of your failure has barreled into me as I attempted to take the afternoon air. I cannot adequately express my disappointment, Duvall, truly I cannot. Ah, good afternoon, Miss Penance. You're looking well. My congratulations on your rapid recovery since this morning. One can only hope your disposition is now as sunny as your appearance."

She placed her fists on her hips. "You let go of that poor, innocent boy this instant, you monster!"

Pierre's social smile remained intact. "Oh dear, I deduce that I have once again raised myself up only to open myself to a fall. Obviously you are to be perpetually tiresome, Miss Penance. But it is of no matter if you are quite set on such a course, as *you* are not my problem. This urchin, however, *is* my concern. Be still, Master Holloway, if you please," he asked of the squirming Jeremy, "as it would pain me to box your ears. Duvall, are you going to allow me to be thwarted in my zeal to accomplish a good deed? If nothing else, please consider the fate of my immortal soul."

Duvall began to wring his hands, his entire posture one of pitiable subservience. "Ask of me to cut off my two hands, good sir, and I will gladly make them a gift to you. Have my tongue to be ripped out with the pincers and served up to the dogs for dinner—order hot spikes to be driven under my fingernails. Anything, dear sir! Anything but, but"—he gestured toward Jeremy—"but this!"

"Come, come, Duvall," Pierre scolded, advancing another step. "Don't be so bashful. How often have I begged you to consider yourself free to express your innermost thoughts? Tell me how you *really* feel. Help him, Miss Penance. Explain to my dear Duvall that he shouldn't keep such a tight rein on his emotions."

Miss Penance, as even she had begun to think of herself, narrowed her eyes as she ran her gaze assessingly up and down the elegantly clad Pierre Standish. "You look better dressed," she said at last, although the tone of her voice did not hint at any great improvement over his banyan and bare, hairy legs. "The only thing remaining to be done to make you passably bearable would be to put a gag in your mouth. You are, Mr. Standish, by and large, the most insufferable, arrogant, nasty creature it has ever been my misfortune to encounter! How dare you maul that poor child that way? How dare you insult this man, who is obviously your slave?"

Ignoring her insults, Pierre honed in on one thing she

had said. "Of *all* the creatures you have met, Miss Penance? May I deduce from this that you have regained your memory? Shall I have Duvall order a celebratory feast?"

Quick tears sprang to her eyes. "How I loathe you, Mr. Standish," she gritted out from between clenched teeth. "No, I have not yet regained my memory, sir. But I *have* met your father, your beleaguered servant, and this poor underfed, persecuted boy—and each of them is twice the man you are. You—you idiotic, conceited *fop!*"

"God's beard! She makes of you a mockery, good sir! It is of the most deplorable!" Duvall exclaimed, taking three steps away from her in order to distance himself from her disparaging words.

Jeremy halted in his struggle to free himself from Pierre's painful grip, his mouth hanging wide as he gasped at Miss Penance. "Dicked in the nob, dat's wot she is," he said at last. "Dat's thanks, ain't it, guv'nor—and atter all yer done fer 'er! Does yer wants me ter level 'er? She's jist m' size, so's it'd be a fair fight."

Pierre looked down on the recently liberated chimney sweep. "I'd rather you allowed Duvall to make you presentable, Master Holloway, if you are cudgeling your brain for a way to express your thanks to me. Duvall? You agree?"

"Ask of me to cut off my two hands, good sir, and I will gladly make them a gift to you. Have my tongue to be ripped out with the pincers and—" Duvall stopped himself, taking a deep breath and squaring his shoulders. "Yes, sir," he ended fatalistically. "Very good, sir."

"You both are so kind, you threaten to unman me," Pierre drawled, a smile lurking in his dark eyes as he looked over to see Miss Penance holding back her fury with an effort. "Please leave us now, before I embarrass myself by falling on your necks in gratitude for your loyalty."

Jeremy and Duvall reached the end of the path before Miss Penance said, her voice measured, "You . . . make . . . me . . . *ill!* I suppose you think *I'm* supposed to be feeling three kinds of a fool for berating you when you are so obviously deserving of my thanks for not allowing me to lie in the road when you discovered me? That is the point of this exercise, is it not? Well, please do not hold your breath waiting for my thanks, for you will only succeed in turning that insufferably arrogant face of yours a hideous purple!"

Pierre walked over to a nearby bench and motioned for her to sit down. "You're right, of course," he agreed, settling himself beside her. "I was the most horrid of selfish creatures to have spirited you away from your so comfortable resting place. How could I have been such a cad? How will you ever forgive me for my callous disregard for your privacy? Shall I order the horses put to immediately, so that I can return you there before bedtime?"

"Don't be any more foolish than you can help. That's not what I meant, and you know it!" she countered, longing to punch him squarely in his aristocratically perfect nose. "Obviously you have somehow rescued Jeremy as well, and probably done something for that poor, nervous Duvall so that he looks upon you as a near god. But if you have some twisted desire to surround yourself with fawning admirers, I'm afraid that in this case you have badly missed the mark. I may have been born, figuratively speaking, only this morning, but I do possess some basic common sense. You could not care less what happens to me. You're only using me in some twisted, obscure way that benefits you, and I have to tell you, I resent it. I resent it most thoroughly! The moment I have recovered my memory I will be more than pleased to wave you a fond farewell as I go out of your life forever!"

"Such a passionate—dare I also mention, lengthy?—speech. You see me prostrate before you, devastated by your eloquent, long-winded vehemence," Pierre drawled, stifling a yawn.

"*Oh!*" she exploded, jumping to her feet. "I can only hope I discover that I *am* a murderess, so I can kill you with a clear conscience!"

Watching as she ran back toward the house, leaving one too-large shoe behind on the gravel path in her haste, Pierre raised his hand to absently stroke the small crescent-shaped scar that seemed to caress his left cheekbone. "Such a darling girl," he mused aloud. "I believe I have been more than justly revenged on my loving father."

Chapter Five

"She's *where!* I don't believe it! I refuse to believe it!" cried a female voice. "Quickly, fetch me my hartshorn. I feel faint!"

"Rubbish. You never faint, for all your moaning. You're strong as an ox," replied her male companion.

"Oxen, always oxen! Have you no other animal to use as a comparison? To think that your last tutor told me you showed an active imagination. It's a good thing I turned him off when I caught him winking at the upstairs maid, or I'd show him an active imagination! And have some pity on your elders. My poor heart could give out at any moment."

"It would be a better job to stop worrying about your heart and begin worrying about your neck! About both our necks."

"Why? We haven't done anything, have we? They can't hang a person for merely *talking* about murder. Besides, it's only her word against ours. Oh, why did she have to end up there? Anywhere but Standish Court. André Standish! He's completely, utterly ruthless. My blood runs cold at the very thought of him. He's so smooth, so mysterious. He seems to know everything."

"It's not the father who worries me. It's the son. I heard all about Pierre Standish when I was in London for the Season. He's like the father, but meaner. Killed his groom, you know—just for saddling the wrong horse. I do wish, though, that my man had his way with a cravat."

"But it has been five days since you went chasing off after her, and nothing has happened. I have been worried to death, waiting for you to return, waiting for the constable to come carry me away to some terrible, smelly gaol. Now you come back here, telling me she's not twenty miles from this wretched hovel you've rented, and with André Standish of all people. How could you have hidden in the bushes, watching the son cart her away like that? What are we going to do when they confront us?''

"Why, we're going to deny everything, of course. It's her word against ours, after all, and besides, no one has been murdered—yet. Of course, there's always the possibility she'll die, for she was unconscious when Standish lifted her into his coach. God, to think that I had finally run her to ground, just to have her bolt away from me into the roadway as we heard a carriage approach. You cannot know how prodigiously I hated hiding in the hedgerow while Standish all but plucked her out of my hands. Yes, it would serve her right to die from the tumble she took. That would solve the problem quite nicely.''

"Then we'd be free of her forever! Oh, that's above everything wonderful. But what if she lives? No, you have to go back to Standish Court. You have to go back, and silence her once and for all.''

"With Pierre Standish there to guard her? And you said you loved me. But you're right. She has to die now, or everything is ruined.''

"Yes, yes, it does present a problem. But we have no choice. Besides, you don't have to leave straight away. It can wait until tomorrow. Sit down, my dear, you look weary. Other than the fact that you couldn't apprehend that dreadful girl, was it a nice trip? The countryside is so pleasing this time of year.''

Jeremy Holloway ran halfway down the length of the shiny black and white tiled foyer in his stockinged feet, an oversized knitted cap pulled down over his ears, then skidded the rest of the way on the slippery floor, whistling through the gap between his front teeth as he held his arms wide to maintain his balance. He quickly held his hands out in front of him before he cannoned into the closed doors to the drawing room.

Grinning from ear to ear in enjoyment of this new amusement, he turned himself about, ready to attack the slippery floor from the other direction, only to feel his shoulders firmly grasped by a pair of strong hands. Looking up—looking a long way up—he saw his new master staring down at him, his left eyebrow arched inquisitively.

"Good morning, Master Holloway," Pierre said quietly. "May I be so bold as to assume you are prepared to explain what you're doing?"

" 'Allo there, guv'nor!" Jeremy chirped brightly, his quick mind working feverishly for an explanation. "Givin' a bit o' polish ter the floor, Oi am. 'Artley, yer pantler, asked me ter, yer see, an' Oi'm jist obligin' 'im—doin' 'im a bit of a favor, like. 'E's been ever so kind ter me, yer understands."

"Ah, yes, dearest Hartley. Wasn't that kind of him— and kind of you. Kind and thoughtful—and utter rubbish. Tell me, Master Holloway. Was it enjoyable?"

Jeremy swallowed hard on the enormous lump in his throat and rolled his eyes as if attempting to discover the nearest exit. "Jist cuff me good an' gets it over, guv'nor," he said at last, as Pierre's hands still held him firmly in place. "Oi can takes it."

"He will do nothing of the sort!" Miss Penance exclaimed militantly from behind Pierre. "Mr. Standish, you will please release that poor child at once. Or have you rescued him from his terrible former life only to beat him yourself?"

Recognizing opportunity when it appeared, Jeremy immediately burst into noisy tears, wrenching himself free of Pierre and immediately burying his head against his latest savior's waist. "Oi didn't mean nothin' by it, 'onest, miss. The floor wuz jist there—yer knows. So pretty, so shiny. Don't let 'im beat me, miss, pleez! Ol' man 'Awkins, 'e beat me all the time."

"Don't you worry, Jeremy. I won't let him so much as lay a finger on you," Miss Penance assured him, her arms wrapped tightly around Jeremy's thin shoulders, her violet eyes glaring at the man she considered to be the bully of the piece. "You're terrible with children, you know," she told Pierre condescendingly.

Pierre, who was always appreciative of outstanding theatrical performances, showed his appreciation now, clapping most politely as he commended softly, "Bravo! Bravo! I tell you both, I am most deeply affected. I don't know whether to toss roses at your feet or go off into the woods and fall on my sword. What a cad I am, what a cold, unfeeling monster! I should be horsewhipped."

"I agree. I might only pray that I can be the one to wield the whip, sirrah!"

"My word, really? Such a Trojan you are, Miss Penance. Is that blood I see in your eyes?"

Jeremy pulled his face free from Miss Penance's smothering embrace to see that the two adults had all but forgotten him as they stared at each other, his female protector with some heat, his male protector with barely suppressed amusement. Clearly his presence was no longer required, and he carefully disengaged his hands from Miss Penance's waist and ran for the safety of the servant's quarters, careful both to pick up his still new shoes and to refrain from sliding as he neared the door that led to the kitchens.

"Now here's a dilemma," Pierre said after a space, his gaze never leaving the shining violet glare that still bore into him. "It would appear, Miss Penance, that the object of our latest contretemps has succeeded in eluding both my cruel, animalistic wrath and your fierce, motherly protection. Do we continue to stand here, staring at each other until one of us crumbles under the strain, or do we agree to a cessation of hostilities—only until the next time, of course—so that I might continue toward the breakfast room without fear of feeling a shaft of cold steel plunge between my shoulder blades?"

Miss Penance, who had already begun to feel rather foolish—not that she for one moment would let that insufferable prig know it!—lowered her chin and stepped back three paces, motioning for Pierre to precede her toward the breakfast room. "Hunger alone makes me accompany you, sir," she told him, then gasped as he took her arm so that they walked together down the hallway to breakfast.

The room was empty of other occupants when they arrived, Miss Penance quickly disengaging her arm from Pierre's grasp as she made for the side table that held an enormous array of hot and cold food. After piling eggs and kippers and toast indiscriminately on her plate, she retreated to the far end of the long dining table and sat down, as far away from Pierre Standish and the coffee pot as she could. After all, it was one thing to share a table with the man. It was asking entirely too much to believe she would pour for him as well.

Putting a forkful of eggs into her mouth—while trying not to notice either the absence of salt or the salt cellar that sat directly in front of Pierre halfway down the table—she lowered her gaze in the hope her long black lashes would disguise the fact that she was staring at him.

There was no denying it, more's the pity, he really was a very nicely set-up man. Thin but well muscled, and taller than she by at least a foot, he wore his clothes well, even if he seemed to wear nothing but whitest white and blackest black. Of course, the white of his cravat showed his tanned skin to advantage, while the black of his clothes almost exactly matched the dead-of-night shade of his hair—which didn't mean that she found him attractive, for she did not.

Of course she didn't.

She lowered her gaze to her plate, somewhat alarmed to see the kippers she had placed there, for she didn't think she was going to like them. They looked so *dead*. Pushing them to one side with her fork, she took a deep breath and lifted another forkful of eggs to her mouth.

"Salt?" Pierre asked just as she closed her mouth around the fork, his voice dripping innocent inquiry.

"No," she snapped, adding, "thank you," only because she knew it was polite to do so. Glaring at him once

45

again—she seemed always to be glaring at him—she stabbed her fork into the food on her plate and took a whopping mouthful of kippers, her eyes immediately widening in shock. "Mmmfff!" she mumbled, knowing that, no matter how unladylike it would be, there was simply no way in the world she was going to swallow the nastiness now filling her mouth.

Pierre, his face determinedly blank, propped his elbow on the table and with chin in palm, inquired sweetly, "Coffee, Miss Penance?"

Her teeth firmly clenched, her lips nearly disappearing as she drew them into a thin line, Miss Penance could only glare at him and shake her head—vehemently. "Mmmfff!" she repeated, tears beginning to sting her eyes.

"I'll take that as a no," Pierre answered amicably. "Perhaps you'd care for a glass of milk? After all, kippers can be very, um, salty."

Her hands digging into the serviette in her lap, she used her tongue to shift the kippers to one side of her mouth, still refusing to chew.

"Not very talkative, are you, Miss Penance. Miss Penance," he repeated, sitting back at his ease. "We have to do something about that name, don't we? I mean, it was all right for a while, but you've been with us for three days now, and to tell the truth, it is beginning to weary me. Have you any suggestions for a replacement?"

The eggs in her stomach—the unsalted eggs in her suddenly unsettled stomach—were threatening to revolt, forcing her to bolt from the room or to dispose of the kippers posthaste, either solution bound to be remarked upon by the still solicitously smiling Pierre Standish.

"Miss Penance, much as I am enjoying this, enough is enough." Pierre rose, reaching for the water pitcher and an empty glass. "Here. What's the matter? Kippers got your tongue?"

That did it! The serviette found its way to her lips and she rid herself of the kippers just as Pierre waved a glass of water in her face. She grabbed it, too grateful to refuse his help, and downed the cool liquid as fast as she could, not caring about anything except ridding herself of the taste of salted herring. "Oh!" she exclaimed, gasping, once the glass was empty. "That was horrid!"

"It's an acquired taste," Pierre told her, sitting down once more. "I believe it is safe to say that you, Miss Penance, have not acquired it."

Using the handkerchief she had unearthed from her pocket to dab at her moist eyes, Miss Penance responded grudgingly, "Apparently not. Thank you. I'll see that the serviette is laundered."

Pierre ignored this last statement, choosing rather to go back to the subject of her name. "I have been giving it some thought," he began, knowing she would have no choice but to follow where he was leading, "and I have decided to call you Miss Addams—as in Adam and Eve, you understand—but with two D's, so as to not be too ordinary. Not being particularly partial to the name Eve, however, I shall leave the matter of your first name entirely to you."

"Well, isn't that too bloody generous of you," the newly christened Miss Addams began furiously. "I'd just as soon you—"

"Your language, Miss Addams, please! Consider my tender ears."

She ignored him, continuing, "I'd just as soon you left the entire matter to me, or to your father, as he has informed me that *he* is to be my guardian until such time as I remember exactly who I am."

"My father, yes. And how is that gentleman? I have not seen him above once since he scolded me for distressing you with the sight of my legs. He warned me that I might have compromised you, but I disabused him of that assumption, considering that you are quite the most uncompromising female I have ever encountered."

"Caroline!"

"I beg your pardon?"

"Caroline. You're not deaf. Dumb?—well, that is arguable, I believe. I wish to be called Caroline. Caroline Addams."

47

"Caroline." Pierre raised his left eyebrow, a mannerism that was becoming increasingly infuriating to Caroline Addams. "That may be an unfortunate choice. Heaven knows it hasn't done Caroline Lamb a world of good. Are you quite settled on it, then?"

She crossed her arms at her waist. "Completely and irrevocably," she declared.

"There is nothing complete or irrevocable in this life, Miss Addams, except our assurance of one day leaving it." Pierre looked down at his plate, realizing he had quite lost his appetite. He rose, carefully pushing in his chair. "Now, if you'll excuse me?"

"Never!" Caroline answered quickly, knowing she was behaving most childishly, but also knowing that she had been provoked. After all, he was the one who seemed to like her best when cast in the role of shrew. "I shall be happy to see you go, but I shall never excuse you."

He stopped, his hand still on the back of the chair, and looked consideringly down the table at her. "You know, Miss Addams," he said, almost as if he was saying the words as he thought them, "I am almost convinced that you are deliberately provoking me."

Caroline's mouth opened wide as she raised her hands to her cheeks in feigned shock. "No! Whatever would make you think that, Mr. Standish?"

He ignored her obvious dramatics. "The question then is: why? Perhaps you are fighting some wild attraction for me? Oh dear, that must be it. It was the legs, wasn't it? Admit it, Miss Addams. I most particularly remember your fascination with my legs. You're mad with love for me."

"I'm what?" she exclaimed, feeling her cheeks beginning to flame. Now he had gone too far. "You're depraved!"

"So I've been told," Pierre admitted, turning to go. "But I've never before heard the accusation voiced in the way of a complaint. Ah, well, I think I shall go now, to beat my devoted valet heavily about the head and shoulders, in order to regain some of my trampled self-esteem.

Good day, Miss Addams. I leave you to enjoy the rest of your delicious meal in peace.''

"And good riddance to him!" Caroline concluded heatedly as Pierre closed the door behind him. So aggravated was she that she vented her anger by giving her serviette a wicked shake, intending to spread it across her knees once again, only to send the rejected bite of kippers skidding across the parquet floor.

A few moments later the sunny breakfast room was entirely empty of human occupation, with only two uneaten plates of rapidly congealing food left behind to show that the room had ever been occupied.

Chapter Six

André looked up from the letter he was penning in the supposed privacy of his study to see his son enter the room, an unusually enigmatic smile on his darkly handsome face. "Have you succeeded in finding something to amuse you, my boy? You look almost pleased. Much as it reveals the weakness of my old age, I must tell you, it's unnerving to observe you so happy."

Pierre settled himself comfortably in an oversized burgundy leather wing chair, draping one long, elegant booted leg over the arm of the chair. "This is not happiness you see upon my face, Father. It is an outward sign of my depravity. I have this on good authority, you understand. Your son is hopelessly, but happily, depraved."

The older Standish signed his name to the bottom of the sheet with his usual flourish and carefully laid down his pen before remarking on his son's nonsense. "You've been teasing our little guest again, haven't you, Pierre? It really is too bad of you. What was it this time? Have you been showing her your legs again?"

"Nothing so daring. I merely told her I've decided on a surname for her. Addams—with two *D*'s of course, to raise her from the ordinary. She, in her turn, linked Addams with Caroline, a mundane but serviceable appellation, barely worthy of a young lady who might well be a missing heiress. Of course, she might just as easily be a fleeing housemaid, which would make her choice of name smack of a pushy young lady dangerously overreaching herself, but I was not so boorish as to point that out to her."

50

"Of course," André answered, rolling his eyes. "You are, if nothing else, discreet."

"I'll ignore that outburst. We were rubbing along together fairly well, Miss Addams and I—except for the kippers, of course—when suddenly, inexplicably, she turned hostile. It wasn't a pretty sight, I can tell you. She is a most highly strung female."

After sanding the letter and then shaking the excess into a small dish, André folded the single heavy ivory vellum sheet and applied a small wax seal. "I refuse to discuss kippers with you, Pierre, no matter how you dangle them before my curiosity. I've just completed a communication to my solicitor in London, requesting that he send us a suitable chaperone posthaste. Shall I amend it, asking him to send me a bodyguard as well, or are you done with trying to drive my anonymous ward out of her wits?"

Pierre lifted a hand to lightly stroke his scarred cheekbone. "Anonymous. The Anonymous Miss Addams. It does have a poetic ring about it, doesn't it? I must have been inspired. I should like the bodyguard, I suppose, although I believe your concern is misplaced. Miss Addams is in no danger from me, but rather the opposite. As a matter of fact, that is why I am here, pestering you in your private sanctum. I do believe I shall be reconvening my remove to London before my poor, abused confidence sustains some irreparable damage from your ward's pointed tongue."

André tapped the folded letter lightly against his chin as he studied his son's negligent pose. "She's routed you then, my son? I grow to like our Miss Addams more with each passing moment."

The left eyebrow that had so infuriated Caroline earlier now moved in a slight upward direction, rather like a silent punctuation of Pierre's thoughts. "Feeling rather full of yourself, aren't you, Father?" Pierre drawled, turning to place both his feet on the floor. "But you couldn't be more wrong. I have responsibilities, you know."

"You do?" André questioned with patent incredulity. "I should deeply appreciate a partial listing of these 'responsibilities,' as I cannot imagine anything more pressing in your life than an appointment with your tailor.''

"Responsibilities," Pierre pursued, undaunted. "I have a household in town that I have been sadly neglecting this past fortnight. I have important papers of some sort or other to sign, or at least I believe I do. It is difficult to keep track of such things. And, oh yes, I have promised Master Holloway that I would return him to his beloved Piccadilly. It's enough that Duvall has cut off all the poor boy's hair and scrubbed him until his nose shines brighter than the sun. I can't disappoint the little scamp now."

André coughed, covering his mouth, and with it, his smile. "You mean to make me believe you are going to toss young Master Holloway straight back into the den of inhuman thieves that first sold him into service? You may be many things, Pierre, but you cannot convince me that you, my only son and light of my life, are stupid."

As Pierre had no intention of returning Jeremy to any woman who would sell him to a sweep for a half a crown, he lowered his eyes, avoiding his father's gaze. "I only mean to have the boy pay a flying visit to the place, seeing his former home from the safety of my carriage. Only then will I be able to resign him to living in the country, surrounded by the lesser evils of clean, fresh air and ample food. The boy has a romantic vision of his former home and hearth that only a good dose of reality can hope to dispel. Then I shall install him at my estate in Surrey, out of harm's way. Now, having bared my soul to you, and only to you, for I wouldn't wish the world to think I have become soft, have I succeeded in reaffirming your fatherly faith in me?''

André crossed the room to look down at his son. "You are being kind, Pierre. Why?''

"Kind, Father? Please. I am never kind. I am merely, to quote you, lending a bit of 'compassionate assistance to one of the helpless wretches of mankind, without a single thought of personal reward.' Did I get that just right, Father? I should so hate to misquote your immortal words of wisdom.''

"You're running away," André announced incontrovertibly, smiling down on his son. "Oh, this is gratifying in the extreme. I'd always hoped to live long enough to see such a day."

"You're dangerously twisted, Father," Pierre warned, rising to his feet. "If I am an unnatural son, you are a most irregular parent. Loving you as I do, I hesitate to point that out, but the need for self-preservation compels me. No, sir. I am not running away. I am leaving. There is a vast difference between the two."

André, his expression serious, only nodded. "I'll bid Miss Addams your farewells for you. I see no need to expose either of you to each other again, considering the adverse effect you seem to have on one another."

"How utterly kind of you," Pierre drawled sweetly. "And shall you hold tight to my hand until I reach the safety of my carriage? Really, Father, you are most hopelessly heavy-handed in this previously untried role of matchmaker. Oh, yes," he said as his father showed signs of protesting. "You are become most sadly lacking in Machiavellian skills, dearest Father, probably just one more damning effect of rapidly encroaching old age. Speaking as one who once stood in awe of your skills, I must tell you, it's a sad, extremely sad, spectacle to witness."

Unruffled by this masterful put-down, André only smiled and said, "Again you overreact, my son. My concern was solely for Miss Addams. I would never think to exhaust myself in order to comfort you."

Pierre bowed, silently acknowledging André's denial. "Your reassurances do comfort me nonetheless. Now, if you'll excuse me, I should like to track down Duvall and make him the happiest man on earth by ordering him to pack. He has never been enamored of the country, you understand, much preferring the hustle and bustle of city life."

André regarded the letter in his hand. "You have just given me an idea. Familiar as I am with your neck or nothing approach to travel, perhaps you will favor me by delivering this missive in person once you reach London, saving me considerable time in my quest for a suitable chaperone for Miss Addams?''

Bowing once more, Pierre answered, "As I live only to bring ease to your declining years, it would be my pleasure to play post boy. I should even be willing to take on the task of ferreting out this suitable chaperone myself, as I have some firm ideas on just what sort of female is needed.''

"You do," André commented blandly. "I should like to hear a list of your specifications.''

"She should be strong, both in back and in heart," Pierre began, ticking off his fingers one by one. "She should have at least a nodding acquaintance with stable speech, so as not to be shocked when Miss Addams's command of polite conversation deserts her. Also, along with the usual virtues of pristine morals, a watchful eye, and no annoying habits—such as picking her teeth with the tines of her fork or ferreting out your private stock of port and commandeering it for herself—she should be at least ten years your senior. I should not wish to exchange one possible compromise for another.''

Now it was André's turn to bow. "You are too kind, my son. Have I neglected to mention that I have instructed cook to prepare rare roasted beef with horseradish sauce for dinner this evening?'' With a slight self-deprecatory grimace and a wave of one elegant hand, he pushed the question aside. "Please forgive me—it was but a momentary lapse.''

Pierre opened his mouth to, his father was sure, graciously accept his apologies—a terribly lowering prospect for one who still considered himself his son's superior when it came to subterfuge—when a shrill female screech interrupted.

"What the devil?'' Pierre exclaimed, already moving toward the open French doors that led straight onto the garden, his father close on his heels.

Caroline Addams's small, muslin-clad body shot into the room. Stopping abruptly, her head still turned partway around, as if trying to catch sight of the demon that was pursuing her, she crashed directly into Pierre's chest. "Ooof!" she exclaimed as her breath left her body, and held tight to Pierre's arms to steady herself.

"Add one more requirement to that list I gave you, please, Father," Pierre said, unruffled. "This chaperone of yours must be extremely fit and fleet of foot if she hopes to keep your Miss Addams in tow. Either that, or might I suggest leading strings?"

Caroline, having recovered sufficient breath to speak, immediately went on the attack. "Unhand me, you idiot!" she demanded, pushing free of his too-familiar clutches, refusing to consider that she might be the cause of their current situation. "And don't just stand there with that stupid, smug smirk on your face! I could have been murdered!"

Pierre's "stupid, smug smirk" remained firmly in place. "Nonsense, my dear Miss Addams with two *D's*. You were in no danger of being murdered. After all, think of it—*I* was nowhere about. Unless, perhaps, you have succeeded in making other enemies during your short sojourn under my father's protection?"

"Sarcasm! Always sarcasm. And bad sarcasm at that," Caroline retorted. "Do you never tire of hearing the sound of your own voice?" She ran over to where André was standing, silently watching and listening to this exchange of unpleasantness between his son and his ward. "Mr. Standish! You believe me, don't you?"

André put a comforting arm around her shoulders and drew her close in what he would have termed a fatherly embrace. "Of course I believe you, my dear," he informed her. "Only one question, if you please. What was it that you said?"

She pulled away from André, no longer frightened but extremely angry. "I was accosted in the gardens, of course," she told them both, looking from one to the other of the Standish's hoping she had shocked them.

"You ran afoul of one of the gardeners?" Pierre suggested, stifling a yawn. "They're very possessive of their greenery. You should really try to keep to the paths, and not trample on the posies.''

"I did not!'' she contradicted defiantly. "I was merely walking down one of the paths—near those delightful shrubberies you showed me yesterday, Mr. Standish,'' she elaborated, turning to André, whom she would much rather speak to and look at, Pierre's silently mocking eyes infuriating her to the point where she knew she would soon lose all control over her nerves. "Suddenly, out of nowhere, there was this—this *man!* He must have been as big as a house! He was looking at me in the most prodigiously speculative way, and he had a large sack in his hand. He took two steps toward me, and I screamed. You may have heard me.''

"Prinny and his court heard you,'' Pierre slid in quietly, "and they're in Brighton, I believe, eating seventeen-course meals and doing whatever else it is they do. You probably disturbed a poacher clumsily plying his trade too close to the house. The poor man is most likely miles from here by now, still running as if all the hounds of hell were after him, and with his hands clapped to his ringing ears.''

Caroline stared at André, trying to gauge his opinion. What she saw was not encouraging. Her arms flapping wildly, like a small, flightless bird, she began swooping about the study, her too large shoes flop-flopping as she went. "You don't believe me—either of you! What must I do to convince you—*die* for you?''

"So dramatic, my dear girl,'' Pierre remarked, looking at his father from beneath lowered lids. André nodded, only slightly, and his son nodded in return, the two reaching out to each other in silent communion. "But I must admit,'' Pierre began carefully, "you do begin to interest me. Tell me about this terrible man with the large sack. Was he more than ten feet tall? Did he drool, or just shoot sparks of blue fire from his one, horrible, bulbous eye?''

Caroline stopped her furious fluttering and subsided heavily into the oversized wing chair Pierre had vacated a few minutes earlier. "Oh, shut up,'' she grumbled, allowing her chin to drop onto her chest. "Mr. Standish,'' she said crushingly, looking up through her long black lashes at André, "I hate to be the one to cause you pain, but I believe your dearest late wife must have somehow played you false. This idiotic ninny cannot possibly be your son, no matter how much he resembles you physically. You have been kindness itself to me, while he is the meanest, most obtuse, self-important, belittling—"

"—beast in nature," Pierre finished helpfully when Caroline seemed to lose her train of thought.

She sat up very straight, the toes of her too big shoes barely touching the floor. "See!" she exclaimed, pointing an accusing finger at Pierre. "Now, you've heard it out of his own mouth! Oh, please, sir, send him away so that I can tell you about the man in the garden."

André shooed Pierre away with a wave of his hand, but his son withdrew no further than the French doors, idly casting his gaze over the garden as he appeared to ignore the occupants of the room. Pouring a small glass of sherry for his ward, André proffered it to her and took possession of the facing wing chair, his elbows on the arms of the chair, his hands elegantly cupped beneath his chin.

"Ignore him, my dear," he told Caroline. "Heaven knows it is difficult, but I have every confidence you can manage it if you try. Now, tell me about this man you saw tippy-toeing about in my garden."

Caroline took a small, tentative sip of the sherry, then downed the rest in one gulp, shivering only slightly at its immediate impact on her system. "With pleasure, Mr. Standish," she said, sitting up very straight. "As I said, I was taking the air in the garden, near the decorative shrubbery, when I heard a noise in the bushes. I looked up just in time to see this man—not nearly so tall as yourself, sir, now that I am no longer in danger and can think more clearly, but still with two eyes and no sign of drool about his mouth—standing not three feet away from me, a large sack held open in both hands, just as if he was preparing to bring it down over my head. He wore a hat pulled down around his ears, so that I couldn't see his face too clearly, but he was very menacing, I'm convinced of that."

"You must have been terrified," André allowed, deftly removing the glass from her hand.

"I was. I said something to him—I don't remember just what—and screamed and ran straight to this room, and the man didn't follow. Now, are you going to do anything about it or not?" she ended, despising the slightly shrill sound of her last question, for she did not like letting either Standish know that she was still frightened. "I mean, if you think anything needs to be done," she added weakly.

"That was a very good explanation, my dear. Very clear, very concise, and very unnerving," André pronounced, looking over to where Pierre was standing, his hands clasped behind his back, still staring into the garden. "What say you about all this, Pierre?"

He turned to face the occupants of the room. "I say, dear Father, that unless we have a remarkably shortsighted poacher who mistook Miss Addams here for a pheasant, then we shall have to investigate this incident most thoroughly. After all, we cannot have a guest in our house disturbed in this way, can we?"

"We, Pierre?" André repeated pointedly, raising his eyebrows. "But I thought you were about to depart for the metropolis. Have you had a sudden change of heart, a rare stab of consideration?"

"Oh, dear," Pierre said, one hand to his heart. "Do you think so? I should hope not. Perhaps I'm sickening for something."

Caroline bounded from her chair, heading for the door to the hallway. "You're sickening all right!" she shot back over her shoulder before slamming the door behind her with a mighty bang.

"I think she's a trifle upset," Pierre remarked placidly, staring at the closed door. "The child's disenchantment with me to one side, however, the fact that we have no clear idea as to who she is begs me to ponder the possibility that she might be correct—and that someone is trying to murder her."

André, careful to conceal his smile from his son, ripped the letter to his solicitor neatly in two and tossed the halves into the cold hearth. "Then you'll be staying to dinner, Pierre? Cook will be most pleased, although I imagine that, conversely, your devoted Duvall will be devastated."

Chapter Seven

It was early in the morning, and the noise of uncooperative horses being put into harness in the courtyard in preparation for another long day on the road filtered through to the common room, where many of the inn's patrons were partaking of their breakfast.

Off in one shadow-darkened corner of the large, low-ceilinged room sat a conservatively dressed couple, by outward appearances and by their signatures on the inn register, mother and son, the two deep in some serious discussion in between taking hearty bites of an equally hearty fare.

"I still don't see why you couldn't have sprung for a private dining chamber," the young man was saying, his thin, sad face wearing a disheartened frown that seemed comfortably at home there. "It's bloody dangerous, sitting out in the open this way, exposing ourselves to anyone who might come through the door."

"I keep telling you not to swear in front of me. Just like your father, aren't you?" the woman retorted around a mouthful of eggs. "Always reaching into my pockets for your own comfort. They are not bottomless, you know. Besides, you worry too much."

"You weren't the one who had to run and scramble for miles and then hide in that thorny thicket yesterday until it was dark," the man grumbled, rubbing at an angry-looking scratch that ran down one side of his face. "She was screaming to wake the dead. I was sure someone was going to clap me on the shoulder at any moment, and haul me off for attempted kidnapping."

"You don't even know if she saw you," the woman pointed out. "A mouse could have run across her toes, setting her off."

"You still think I'm lying, don't you? You think I never went to the Standish house at all, but only sat in the bushes somewhere all day, out of harm's way, before coming back to you with some moonshine story about nearly being caught. That's mighty unloving of you, do you know that?"

"Then she just mustn't have seen you clearly, dearest," the woman conceded, seeing that the young man's bottom lip was trembling, as if he were close to tears. "You were wearing a hat. And don't pout. Your face might freeze that way. Mother believes you. You said you were half hidden behind the ornamental shrubbery. Yes, she didn't see you clearly, that's the only logical explanation. You'll just have to try again. Pass me one of those delicious-looking biscuits, if you please. The food here is quite remarkably fine for such an out of the way place, don't you think?"

The biscuits were passed, along with a small crock of fresh creamed butter that was the private pride of the innkeeper of the Scarlet Cow, who would have blushed to the top of his bald pate if he could have heard this great praise. "Didn't see me? Damn it! What does it take to convince you? We've been over this a dozen times. Then why did she set to screeching like a greased pig in a trap and go haring off back to the house as fast as her two legs could carry her? Answer me that if you can, you daft woman!"

"Your language, please. Don't break my heart. But it *doesn't* make sense. If she had seen you, the two of us would be before the local constable at this very moment, trying to explain our way out of the hangman's noose. It wouldn't have taken that frightening André Standish a full day and night to ferret us out, seeing as how we're strangers, and staying at this inn not two miles distance from his front door. Why hasn't she cried rope on us? Knowing her, I'm sure she would delight in seeing our necks stretched."

"More to the point—why did she look at me so blankly and then ask me who I am? Anyone would think the chit didn't recognize me. Either that, or she's more of a cool fish than we thought and is running some rig of her own, to get revenge on us, as it were. Kindly leave one of those biscuits for me, if you please."

"A rig of her own? Don't be silly, she's only a girl, and hasn't the wit. No, it can't be that. Perhaps she was just shocked by your sudden presence, and forgot your name for a moment."

"Forgot my name? You named me Ursley, Mother, remember? *Ursley!* A person doesn't forget a name like that. God knows I can't. I couldn't even be called by any other name than Ursley. Not Diccon, or Billy, or even Georgie. You cursed me when you gave me this name, and I shan't ever forget it."

"It is a family name, and very distinguished, or at least it was until your dearest father so carelessly botched our last endeavor—bless his dear, departed soul and may I be forever grateful that the poison I chose did not cause him to suffer unduly." She buttered another biscuit. "I dislike seeing this pettish streak in you, Ursley. Have you been getting quite enough sleep these past few days? And, if you'll remember, your classmates called you Stinker at school. Surely that qualifies as a pet name?"

Ursley ignored his mother's casual mention of her murder of his father by way of a gooey strawberry tart laced with arsenic, for he saw nothing wrong in it, as the man had become an embarrassment to all of them. The only thing that worried him was that he himself was in danger of going down to defeat himself in their current project. It was a thought that could destroy a man's appetite and make him overly anxious to succeed.

He took refuge from his thoughts in another attack. "If you had wished to help me compile a list of grievances against you, Mother, the name Stinker would come second on my list. First of course, is the problem of our little eavesdropper. And I still say she didn't recognize me. I think she must have hit her head as she fell onto the roadway that first time I was chasing her, and can't remember anything."

Ursley's mother thoroughly chewed the last biscuit and swallowed. "Yes, I have heard of strange things like that occurring after an injury to the head. I'll agree that you have a point that bears investigation—though, of course, whether this new development will help or further complicate matters remains to be seen. Let me think on it until it's time for luncheon. There must be some way we can be sure. Perhaps we shall not have to kill her after all. Having her insane and locked up snugly in some asylum would be equally as lovely as having her dead, and quite less the bother."

"And live in constant terror that someday she'll wake up screaming 'That horrible man, Ursley Merrydell, and his wicked mother are trying to murder me?' Oh, no, madam, I should think not!"

"No, no. *I* should think not, as well. But we're going to have to be very careful. If only we could find some way to get ourselves into the Standish household. You know, that is a male household. It would be a shame if the girl's reputation should suffer irreparable damage just because there is no good woman in the house to protect it, don't you think, Ursley? I am a very good chaperone, thanks to your father's unforgivable failure to leave us reasonably provided for, and have impeccable references. Go take a walk to settle your meal, dearest, while I think on this a bit longer, and we'll talk again over luncheon. I wonder . . ."

Caroline had lain awake in her bed for half the night, racking her brain for some elusive memory, some forgotten fact, some small, enlightening clue that might serve to help her rediscover her identity. When the morning came she had nothing to show for her pains except slightly puffy eyes and a lingering headache. A headache that was about to become much worse.

She approached the sunny breakfast room warily—hoping to avoid bumping into Pierre, who would most cer-

tainly destroy her appetite with his unnerving presence—
and succeeded in dining in solitary splendor. It was just
as she was touching the fine white linen serviette to her
lips one final time that the sound of a carriage moving off
down the drive came to her ears.

Idly curious, and hoping against hope that Pierre had
once more changed his mind and was already on his way
to London—and out of her life—she drifted into the drawing room to see that same infuriating man standing at the
mantel, dressed in his usual impeccable black and white,
frowning over a missive he held in one hand.

"Bad news?" she ventured softly, hoping against hope
that he had just learned his horses had all lost at the races
and his cook had run off with the upstairs maid, taking all
his silver plate with them. "You look faintly downpin,
although I have found, with your usually unreadable expressions, it is difficult to tell just what is going on inside
that head of yours—if, indeed, anything does."

"Ah, Miss Addams. You're awake, and as full of compliments as ever." Pierre unhurriedly folded the letter he
had been reading, pocketed it in his jacket, and turned to
look at his father's ward. She was coming more into her
looks with each passing day, a thought that did little to
change his opinion of her. Pretty is as pretty does, someone had once said, and Miss Caroline Addams had been
remarkably unpretty in her treatment of him. Not that he
cared one way or the other what her opinion of him was,
he reminded himself with a slight mental jolt.

Her midnight hair was once more a cascading tumble of
curls, reminding him of the way she had looked that first
morning when Hartley had startled her from her slumbers
and he had burst into her chamber, hairy legs and all. How
could something so angelically beautiful, so fragilely constructed, so infinitely appealing, be such an unremitting
pain in the—

"You will be devastated to hear the news, I imagine,"
he said, bursting into speech before he could finish his last
thought. "My dearest father has seen fit to desert us."

"What! He couldn't have! He wouldn't have!" Caroline looked to the window, as if she could see the carriage that had recently pulled away and somehow call it back, then over to Pierre, her quick mind registering the fact that he appeared mildly pleased at her nearly hysterical reaction to his news. She cleared her throat, folding her hands together at her waist. "I see," she said, striving to be calm. "A family emergency, no doubt? Perhaps he knew he could not stay under the same roof as you any longer without succumbing to the urge to strangle you?"

"Strangle me? My own father?" Pierre motioned to a nearby chair, politely inviting her to seat herself so that he could do the same.

"Yes," she said, spreading her skirts around her as she chose a chair as far away from him as possible. "Don't feign surprise. I imagine you inspire that sort of feeling in most of your acquaintances."

"Don't judge everyone else's reactions by your own, Miss Addams. I am quite well thought of by many people, unbelievable as that might seem to you."

"I'm not speaking of your paramours, Mr. Standish," Caroline countered smoothly, then gave a silent gasp at the lengths to which her impudent tongue could take her when she was in his company.

Pierre smiled. Her looks improved even more when she was flustered. "We could sit here all morning, listening to you tear strips off my consequence, but I believe we have other matters to discuss. My father, by way of this letter he left before sneaking out of the house like some mischievous youth embarking on a spree, has charged me with your welfare while he travels to London on some trumped-up excuse about how he needs to personally choose a suitable chaperone for you. He is as transparent in his motives, I'm afraid, as a pane of freshly scrubbed window glass."

"His motives?" Caroline asked, not liking the way Pierre was looking at her. He was entirely too familiar in his speech, and always had been, which was bad enough, but now he was looking at her in a way that made her wish she could throw her hand protectively across her breasts, hiding herself from his too observant eyes.

"Father would like it immensely if we were to tumble into love, Miss Addams," Pierre said baldly, not seeing any reason to dress the thing up in fine linen. As a rule, he disliked being obvious, but his father was forcing his hand.

"With each other?" she squeaked, knowing her eyes were as wide as saucers.

"No, Miss Addams," Pierre returned suavely. "I am to fall madly in love with the tweeny, that charming bird-brain servant who bursts into giggles each time I happen to pass her in the hallway, and you are to have your heart stolen away by my so-estimable man, Duvall. And here I have always prided myself on my lucidity. I thought I was being so clear. Please forgive me."

Caroline was on her feet in a flash, wishing she was a man so that she could call this smug, maddening man out and then run him through. That alternative not being open to her, she walked purposefully across the room and leaned down to go eye to eye with him. "Don't . . . be . . . facetious!" she said, punctuating each word with a sharp stab of her index finger against his pristine white shirt-front.

As she jabbed her finger the last time, Pierre lifted his right hand and neatly grabbed her wrist, pulling her down to within inches of his face. "Don't . . . be . . . stupid," he warned silkily, his black eyes flashing dangerously as his smile chilled her to the bone. He held her prisoner for another moment, an eternity during which she more than realized how vulnerable she was, before releasing her as abruptly as he had captured her.

She quickly retreated to her own chair, subsiding into it before her knees, curiously wobbly, buckled completely. "I—I'm sorry," she said, shaking her head. "I don't know what's come over me. I'm not usually so forward."

Pierre did not miss the implication of this last statement. Perhaps he had somehow, accidentally, jiggled her memory. "You're not, Miss Addams? Tell me, please. How can you be so sure?"

A sudden vision of herself not more than a year younger than she was now, dressed in a rather low-cut white gown and laughing delightedly as she went down the dance with some scarlet-jacketed lieutenant flirting for all she was worth, flashed into her mind. "Oh, dear Lord," she breathed, all color leaving her face as she pressed her hands to her cheeks. "You were right about me. I *am* a strumpet!"

Pierre folded his hands beneath his chin, much as his father had done the day before while Caroline told them about the intruder in the garden. "I must tell you, Miss Addams, my mind begins to boggle with your every new revelation. First you regale us with tales of bogeymen in the greenery, and now you confess to being a fallen woman. Tell me, are you an accomplished strumpet, do you suppose, or only a recent practitioner of the oldest profession? You barely seem old enough to have been plying your trade for any great length of time."

Caroline closed her eyes, feeling slightly queasy, and the picture in her mind reappeared. She could see the entire ballroom now, and even make out one or two faces other than her own. It was a lovely ballroom, if slightly rustic, the sort of room to be found in a smaller city, although how she knew that she couldn't remember, and the people looked to be highly respectable—even stuffy. A woman dressed all in purple, and with a most uncomplimentary silver turban banding her head, was regarding her in a clearly condemning way, as if she heartily disapproved of her conduct.

She squeezed her eyes tightly shut, scrunching up her entire face—bringing a genuine smile to Pierre's face at the sight of her wrinkled-up nose—hoping for more, hoping to hear bits and pieces of conversation, for it would seem that she was talking to her dancing partner. The image visible inside her closed eyelids wavered slightly, distorting the disapproving, turbaned lady's face most grotesquely, and then was gone, as quickly as it had come.

She opened her eyes. "I'm not a strumpet," she said softly and to no one in particular, relief clearly evident in her voice. "I'm only distressingly forward, if the ugly purple lady is to be believed."

"I can't know how you feel on the subject, but for myself, I've never put much credence in ugly purple ladies," Pierre supplied helpfully, rising leisurely to his feet. Crossing the room to the drinks cabinet, he poured Caroline a small glass of sherry and delivered it to her. "I shouldn't like for this imbibing of spirits to become a habit, Miss Addams, but I think you could do with a small restorative. May I take it you've had a flash of memory?"

Caroline shook her head, declining the drink, then nodded. "I saw myself at a country ball, flirting most prodigiously with some lieutenant as we went down the dance, shocking the purple lady with my forwardness," she told him, almost immediately regretting having shared the memory with him. "It was not really helpful, as I recognized nothing of the scene save my own grinning face. There wasn't even any music. If only I could call the scene back again, and try to move it past that moment in the dance."

She felt Pierre's hand on her arm, and was startled by the gentleness his touch conveyed, a gentleness so in contrast with his usual condescending treatment of both her and her plight. "Don't push, Miss Addams. There are ways and there are ways. Small, unexpected flashes of memory are only one of them. By one method or another your past will be revealed to you. In the meantime, as Cervantes said: 'Patience, and shuffle the cards.' "

" 'There is a strange charm in the thoughts of a good legacy, or the hopes of an estate, which wondrously alleviates the sorrow that men would otherwise feel for the death of friends.' My goodness! Where did *that* come from?" Caroline exclaimed, amazed at the words from Cervantes's *Don Quixote* that she had just quoted.

"My congratulations, Miss Addams," Pierre murmured, looking down on her. "You become curiouser and curiouser. That you know Miguel de Cervantes's work is surprise enough. Your choice of quote, however, is considerably more than mildly intriguing.''

Caroline brightened. "Yes. Yes, it is, isn't it? What do you suppose it means?''

Pierre lightly stroked the scar on his cheekbone with the smallest finger of his left hand. "I believe it means that you have had a difficult morning and should indulge yourself in a small lie-down in your chamber like a good child. Now, if you'll excuse me, I believe my father's defection leaves me with the sure-to-be fatiguing bother of having to discuss tonight's menu with cook.''

"That's it? That's all you have to say?'' Caroline hopped to her feet, longing to stomp her foot in disgust, refraining only because Pierre was sure to comment on this display of immaturity and at last succeed in maddening her past the point of all rational thought.

Pierre turned back to her, his expression politely inquiring, "You want more?'' he asked solicitously before producing a bored grimace. "Of course, how boorish of me. I seem to have temporarily mislaid my manners.'' He bowed deeply, mockingly, from the waist. "Good morning to you, Miss Addams. As I will be lunching with father's steward, I pray that, after you have sufficiently recovered in the privacy of your chamber, you will enjoy the remainder of your day until we meet again at dinner.''

Caroline watched, openmouthed and silently seething, until Pierre had sauntered from the drawing room, then headed straight to her chamber, exiting it not fifteen minutes later, clad in Eleanore Standish's altered riding habit, the too-large boots clomping heavily against the stairs she took at a rapid pace. She didn't know if she was a good horsewoman, or even if she had ever ridden in the first place, but she'd rather break her neck clearing a five-barred gate than bow to the autocratic Pierre Standish's highhanded direction of her life!

Chapter Eight

She was halfway to the stables before realizing that the day was much too pretty to be spent thinking about either André Standish's defection or the maddening Pierre Standish and his obvious wish to make her life as uncomfortable as possible. She would be happy today, if only to make him miserable!

Her furious pace immediately slackening to a leisurely stroll, Eleanore Standish's intricately braided leather riding crop slapping softly against her skirts, Caroline took a deep breath of fresh country air into her lungs and looked about at the gloriously landscaped grounds that made up a small part of the vast Standish holdings. All at once her fingers began to tingle as she longed for her brushes, wishing to capture the scene with the watercolors from her paintbox.

"I paint!" she said out loud, halting in her tracks as the realization that she had discovered something else about herself penetrated her brain. "Ladies paint. Ladies, and the daughters of good houses. I dance, even if I do flirt. I dance, I paint, and I can quote Cervantes." Her smile was as brilliant as the late morning sun. "I *am* a Somebody!"

Her happiness was fleeting. "Of course, a governess must also know those things," she pointed out to herself as she continued toward the stables. "A governess, or a schoolmistress. No. I'm too young to be a schoolmistress. A governess is possible, even if the thought of being one is terribly lowering. But would a governess dance? No wonder the purple lady was frowning. I probably overstepped myself while supposedly chaperoning her daughters—two of them, and both as uninspiring as their mother, no doubt—and got myself turned off for my pains, without a reference. I've been wandering the world on my own ever since, with neither family nor friends to ease my plight, until I finally got myself into a scrape that ended with me lying facedown in the roadway, dressed in a man's cloak, and minus my shoes. How thoroughly depressing.''

'' 'Ey! Yer al-ays prate ter yerself? Sumthin' havey-cavey 'bout folks who jaw bang when nobody's there ter 'ear 'em.''

Caroline stopped walking and looked around until she discovered the source of the voice that had interrupted her imaginings. She found it sitting perched atop a granite pedestal that supported a lovely statue of a Grecian maiden pouring water into the small, stone-edged pool that surrounded the statue like a miniature moat.

"Jeremy Holloway!'' she exclaimed in relief, for it wouldn't have done for Pierre to have overheard her romantic imaginings or she would never, she was sure, hear the end of it. Waving to Jeremy gaily, she redirected her steps until she was in front of the pool. Sitting down on the low stone wall at the water's edge, she looked inquiringly at the young sweep. "What are you doing here? Did you wade across? I thought you detested Adam's ale.''

He ignored her questions, seemingly more concerned with her welfare. "They'll takes yer away an' fix yer up wit yer own straight-waistcoat iffen yer keeps it up, yer knows that, don't yer? Oi lifted the blunt from a gentry mort an' went ter see the loonies in Bedlam onct on a Sunday. There's all manner of dicked-in-the-nob folks locked up inside, all jist singin' and dancin' and talkin' ter themselves nineteen ter the dozen. Ain't a pretty sight, Oi tell yer. Yer'd best be careful.''

"Thank you, Jeremy, for the advice. I'll do my best not to let that happen to me.'' Caroline allowed her fingertips to dangle in the cool water, trying to catch the ever-widening ripples caused by the water pouring from the Grecian maiden's stone pitcher. "How are you now, Jeremy, now that your active citizens have been routed?''

she asked, careful to keep her gaze diverted from the boy's all-but-bald head until he could replace the knitted cap he constantly wore.

"Oi wuz jist lookin' at m'self in the water," he mumbled, carefully pulling the cap down over the light golden fuzz that barely covered his head. "Oi'm goin' ter kill dat frog, yer know," he added matter-of-factly. "Oi bit 'im good, but Oi'm still goin' ter kill 'im. 'E deserves it, Oi'm thinkin'."

"I understand," Caroline returned sympathetically. "But it had to be done. There's no other way to rid yourself of the pesky little creatures, unfortunately. Your hair will soon grow back, twice as thick and long as before. But must you really kill him, Jeremy? Guv'nor will be grievously saddened, you know, for Duvall is the only person in the world, save you, who can tolerate him."

"Guv'nor likes the froggie?" Jeremy sounded dubious, understandably depressed by what he could only see as a serious flaw in his otherwise perfect savior. "Well, mebbe Oi'll only 'urt 'im bad."

Caroline suppressed a grin and nodded her agreement with this generous concession on the sweep's part. "That's very kind of you, Jeremy," she told him. "Now, would you like to accompany me to the stables? I have a wish to see if I can ride."

As Jeremy's face twisted into an expression of wary incomprehension, Caroline held out her hand, helping him to leap from the pedestal to the wall to the ground, then explained her predicament as they walked together.

"So you see," she ended as Jeremy lifted the latch that allowed them to push back a section of fence and enter the yard, "I have absolutely no memory of anything about myself, other than those few things I just told you."

She felt Jeremy's hand take hold of her's. "Oi'll 'elp yer," he told her, his protective urges coming to the fore. "It's a terrible thing, bein' away from all yer know. That's 'ow Oi wuz when 'Awkins took me."

Caroline felt the back of her throat stinging with emotion as she looked into the boy's open, childish face.

"Thank you so much, Jeremy, for understanding. You have no idea what it means to me to—oh! Jeremy, just look at him! Isn't he a beauty?"

The horse being led into the stable yard was no more than three years old, a huge, sleek, black satin creature with a wide white blaze running the length of his handsome, intelligent face. His form was fluid, hinting of speed even as he was walked slowly in a wide circle, his muscles rippling along his strong flanks, his ears and tail nervously twitching at the sound of Caroline's voice.

Jeremy stopped short in his tracks, eyeing the huge horse warily. "A beauty, is it? 'E looks like a bleedin' devil ter these peepers."

"Nonsense." She approached the stallion fearlessly, taking the reins from the startled groom. Stroking the horse's velvety nose, Caroline murmured fulsome compliments to his handsomeness, then allowed him to nuzzle her open palm. "Sugar, Jeremy," she said, still using the same soothing tone. "Ask the groom for some sugar. This darling creature and I have got to get to know each other."

After doing her bidding, Jeremy approached the stallion gingerly and all but flung the sugar lump at Caroline before quickly scurrying away for, being a child of the city, he had long ago learned to keep his frail body a safe distance from deadly hooves. "The groom says 'is moniker is Obtuse, wotever that means. Be careful-like. 'E looks like a killer iffen Oi ever seen one."

"He doesn't mean it, sweetheart," Caroline assured the horse, feeding it the sugar. "You're just a great big baby, aren't you, Obtuse? Obtuse. You have to be Pierre's mount. No one else would think to saddle you with such an unsuitable name."

As if to confirm her thought, the groom came up to her and told her that Mr. Pierre was most protective of his horseflesh, horseflesh that had been left in the groom's charge, and now that the young miss had petted the horse—and this next bit he would appreciate very much—perhaps she'd be willing to give him back into his hands.

"I have Mr. Pierre's generous permission to ride Ob-

73

tuse,'' she lied with a quick coolness that surprised even her, looking directly into the groom's eyes as she uttered the blatant untruth. ''Please see that he is saddled for me immediately.''

There are many things a groom can do on his own with his master's horse. He can curry the horse, feed the horse, exercise the horse, and even get kicked in the rump by the horse if he isn't careful. All this and more can a groom do on his own. There are some things he cannot do. He cannot buy or sell the horse, beat the horse, or even get bucked off the horse, as he may not mount the horse without his master's permission.

But there is a higher rule, one that the groom knew stood head and shoulders above the rest. He cannot, under pain of instant dismissal, contradict a guest. Caroline, dragging this bit of knowledge from the depths of her memory, knew it as well, and her triumphant smile blighted the man with its brilliance.

Obtuse was fitted with a sidesaddle, and within five minutes Caroline was on his back, galloping out of the stable yard with the nervous, grumbling groom riding behind them on a mount that could not hold a candle to the stallion's speed.

''I can ride!'' Caroline shouted delightedly into the wind that was rushing by her as Obtuse headed for the open field. ''I can ride!''

He rode like a man possessed, quietly cursing the groom who had come pelting back to the stables, having lost Caroline somewhere in the dense trees.

He cursed the soft ground that slowed his mount's progress and the mount itself for not being the more fleet-footed Obtuse.

He cursed his father for having saddled him with the responsibility of someone else's welfare and for that same man's premeditated defection.

But most of all he cursed Caroline Addams, the willful, headstrong idiot of a girl who had ridden off over the countryside without a thought to the danger she might well find there.

Pierre urged his mount into a full gallop, hoping against hope that he would find Caroline still in one piece. "So that I might have the pleasure of killing her myself," he declared through gritted teeth.

She was in danger, he just knew it. No stranger to peril, he had long ago recognized its smell, its chilling effect on his bones, its capacity to swoop down and destroy everything in its path. He had met danger face to face on the Peninsula, slept with it lying by his side, fought with it on more battlefields than he cared to recall, and watched its victims being sucked down into the greedy Spanish mud.

To look at him, Pierre appeared to be a gentleman giving his horse its head, for his impatience was rigidly controlled, a lesson learned long ago. It was an inward battle he was fighting now or, more clearly, two battles, one with his old enemy, danger, and another, even more terrifying, that raged between his heart and his head.

His head told him that Caroline Addams was the last, absolutely the very last person in the world who should matter to him. His heart, beating hurtfully in tune with his mount's galloping hooves, fought to tell him that Caroline Addams was the only person in the world who could ever really matter to him.

Suddenly, just as he pulled his horse to a skidding, plunging halt at the crest of a slight hill in order to scan the horizon, he spied Obtuse tied to a branch of a small tree, a grazing grey gelding tied beside him. His rapidly pounding heart stopped in mid-argument before beginning to beat rapidly again, now more in fear than in anger. Caroline was nowhere to be seen.

Dismounting, and checking to be sure that his pistol was still tucked into his waistband at his back, he proceeded slowly, his eyes scanning the open field and border of trees, his ears alert.

"Oh, Sir John, really?" he heard after a moment, his entire body swinging about at the sound of Caroline's voice, followed by the lilting song of her delighted laugh. "Admit it, sir, you're funning me. Nobody could be that contrary, not even Pierre Standish."

"It's true, I swear it," came a male voice, obviously belonging to the unseen Sir John. "He has always been an odd duck. You can never know what he is thinking."

"But to cut a man dead on Bond Street just because he didn't like the style of his jacket? And the man actually broke down and *cried?* It sounds so incredibly silly."

Pierre pushed back the branches of a wild flowering bush and stepped into the small clearing to see Caroline sitting at her ease on a fallen log, Sir John Oakvale lying at her feet, one hand propped against his cheek.

She looked beautiful sitting there, her entire blue velvet clad figure softly dappled by sun and shade, her expression one of delight, the disapproving frown she customarily donned while in his presence nowhere in evidence. Her smile, the same innocently devastating smile he had glimpsed that first morning of their acquaintance, was now directed at Sir John Oakvale.

Pierre sensed danger again, this time emanating from himself, whom he knew to be capable of falling on Sir John and beating the grinning nodcock into a bloody pulp. He carefully schooled his features into their usual faintly bored expression.

"Hardly silly, Miss Addams," Pierre drawled, masterfully containing himself and stepping completely into the clearing. "The man was utterly crushed, as well he should have been, for I am known to be a most demanding arbiter of the best fashions. He retired to his estates that same day, a broken man, so that I could not tell him that the whole thing was my fault. I had gotten a bit of smut in my eye, you understand, so that in actuality I had passed by him without seeing him. You did remember to tell her that, didn't you, Oakley?"

Sir John scrambled to his feet, hastily brushing dirt and leaves from his buckskins. "Standish!" he exclaimed, looking as guilty as a young lad caught with his hands in the honey pot. "We didn't hear you ride up. And it's Oak-

vale," he added pettishly, wishing he could refrain from correcting Pierre but unable to restrain himself.

"Of course it is, Oakmont. How could I be so forgetful? Do forgive me," Pierre said silkily, walking over to Caroline and extending his hand to her. "You have been very naughty, haven't you, Miss Addams. My groom is quite destroyed by your capriciousness. I left him in the stable yard, a shadow of his former self, as he is sure you are dead and I shall blame him. Or was it that he was sure Obtuse was dead, and I shall demand his life in forfeit? Yes, I'm convinced it was the latter. Only the loss of my dearest Obtuse could serve to put me in a rage."

"My loss would doubtless be cause for a celebration, isn't that correct, Mr. Standish?" Caroline asked, ignoring his hand and rising without aid.

"I shall leave that determination to your own judgment," Pierre offered magnanimously.

"Of course you will. I shall apologize to your groom, for it is my fault he is upset. Your sensibilities and their condition are your own problem, thank goodness, and I care not whether they have or haven't suffered permanent damage. Sir John," she said, walking over to where that man stood, looking about to bolt for the safety of the trees, "it was so very nice to meet you. Perhaps you shall agree to visit me at the Standish home, in order to help me pass these long, tedious days?"

Sir John blushed from his intricately tied cravat to the roots of his wavy blond hair, pleased that Caroline had found his company entertaining. Heaven only knew his father didn't, which was why he had been out riding in the first place, finding that being away from home for as many hours as possible during his duty visits to that same home was less taxing on his easily overset nerves.

Sir John, young, boyishly handsome, and a great pet of the London ladies, who found his company pleasant without being threatening, had come upon Caroline in the field separating his father's small holding from the larger Standish estate. The sight of her had gone a long way toward reconciling him to his enforced visit home, even if the thought that he would have to endure the sure to be uncomfortable presence of Pierre Standish whenever he called on Miss Addams was distasteful to him.

Bowing over Caroline's hand, Sir John said brightly, "I should be honored to visit you, Miss Addams."

Pierre, one foot perched on the fallen log, raised a hand to stifle a yawn. "I had a premonition you would say just that, you dear man, and in just that way. How utterly deflating. I suppose you'll expect me to serve as host, in my father's absence. Oh, very well. Mapletree, please, consider my father's home your home, for the duration."

"That's *Oak*tree!" Caroline fumed, hands on hips, knowing Pierre was taking great pains to get Sir John's name wrong, an insult so blatant she was surprised he would sink to it, for his cuts were usually more subtle.

Sir John coughed slightly and cleared his throat. "Actually, Miss Addams, it's Oak*vale*," he corrected apologetically. "For myself, I don't mind, but Father is rather starchy about people getting it right."

"As well he should be! It's a lovely name," Caroline responded, horrified by her mistake even as she caught Pierre's gaze and found the corners of her lips twitching as a silent message of shared humor flashed between them. Her expression hardened, for she was angry with herself at even this small intimacy with a man she loathed. "Mr. Standish, I've just had a thought."

"You have, Miss Addams? Might I convey my congratulations?" Pierre cut in, seemingly occupied with removing a spot of dust from his brilliantly shined boots. "I refuse further comment, as it would be beneath me."

"Really?" Caroline retorted, obviously not believing him for a moment. "I would have thought you beneath nothing. To continue, sir; if you are not ready to return to the estate, Sir John can bear me company home."

Pierre removed his foot from the log and took a firm grip on Caroline's upper arm. "Much as I detest denying Sir John this opportunity to ingratiate himself with me by performing this kindness, I feel that, as your host, I must cut short my own pleasure and escort you safely back to the stables. My dear fellow, excuse me, but you do understand—don't you, Oakvale?''

So pleased was Sir John that Pierre had deigned to use his correct name, he acquiesced immediately, causing Caroline's upper lip to curl in disdain as he bowed once more over her hand and departed before Pierre could ruin the moment with another of his crushing remarks.

''And now, madam,'' Pierre said softly as they watched Sir John ride away, his tone so mild that Caroline had no idea of what was to come, ''if it isn't an out-of-the-way demand, and putting momentarily to one side your heartless disregard for my groom as well as your kidnapping of Obtuse, do you think you could possibly explain your reasons for deliberately putting yourself in danger?''

Chapter Nine

"Danger? What danger are you talking about, Mr. Standish?" Caroline questioned hotly, immediately going on the offensive. "Oh, just a moment. *Could it be? Is it possible?* Surely you cannot be referring to the 'shortsighted poacher' in the garden? That man, whose presence you did not even choose to investigate by exerting yourself to the point of making an actual search for him, in the unlikely chance I may have been correct and the fellow *was* trying to kidnap or murder me? That man, whose presence in your garden, on your property, was so innocent that your father, who has set himself up as my guardian, has taken himself off to parts unknown, leaving a worthless dandy like you as my only protector? Please, please, good sir, enlighten this poor, confused lady. Is that the *danger* to which you are referring so obliquely?"

"That's the way, Miss Addams. Be nasty," Pierre urged reassuringly. "It's good for the soul. Rage at me, and don't forget a single insult. We, both dissolute father and reprobate son, have done just as you say. We have treated you as if you were naught but an infant, pooh-poohing your fears and not giving your story of the man in the garden the credit you are convinced it deserves."

Caroline was not mollified, as she was certain he did not want her to be. He was smooth. He had only agreed that he and André had not believed her, not that they had been wrong. He was never serious, but constantly flippant, and most incisively cutting. Well, she would not rise to his bait and give him the satisfaction of seeing her lose her temper. If he thought he could push her, she would show him she was capable of pushing back.

"I am pleased to see you have finally decided to believe me," she answered sweetly, just as if she had taken his words to heart, carefully removing her arm from his grasp and heading for her mount. "If your presence at this moment is a belated show of concern, I shall accept your apology."

"I didn't offer one," Pierre pointed out, making a cup of his joined hands and giving her a mounting step to help her into the saddle. "But, then, you already know that, don't you? I merely listed a few Standish failings. Personally, I'm rather proud of them. And, you must admit, your own behavior begs another question. Would a prudent woman ride out alone if she was really convinced she was in danger?"

He had her there, not that she would give him the satisfaction of agreeing with him. She looked down at him from atop Obtuse, knowing she was going to regret her next question. "If you don't believe me about the man, then why did you say I was in danger in the first place? You make precious little sense, Mr. Standish."

"Call me Pierre, Caroline. I think we have outlived the need for such formalities. You're riding my horse, for one thing, a horse that has known none but me on his back, surely a sign that you feel you know me well enough to make free with my possessions. Also, we should remember that we have seen each other in a state of undress. Yes, I would say the time for formalities has passed."

"Answer the question, *Pierre*," Caroline gritted, wondering why she stood here listening to his nonsense, when it would be so easy, so very easy, to spur Obtuse into an instant gallop and leave the insufferable man in the dust. "You did think I was putting myself in danger by riding out alone because of the man I saw in the gardens. That's why you came after me. Admit it."

"I could, I suppose, say that you may have unconsciously put yourself in some peril from some unknown gentleman set on doing you harm. I could say it, but I won't, for I don't believe it."

Caroline could have burst into tears. She was right. He still didn't believe her! He was deliberately leading her on, making her think he was concerned for her safety—concerned for *her*. He didn't care two sticks for her! It was his horse he had come after, and now he was just getting some of his own back, leading her on with all this talk about danger, because he felt she deserved punishment. "I could detest you with very little effort," she said meanly, glaring down at him. *"Very* little effort."

Pierre placed a hand on his heart. "Please, Caroline, your vehemence threatens to crush me." Before she could answer, or even think of something vile enough to say that would do justice to the way she felt at this obvious untruth, his hand moved, delivering a sharp slap to Obtuse's flank, and she was fully occupied in controlling the stallion as it began to race back to the stables.

Several minutes later, as the groom helped her from the saddle, Pierre rode into the yard on his slower mount, tipping his hat to her. "How could you have done that?" she yelled to him. "I could have been killed!"

"As much as I dislike explaining myself, I shall answer you. If you weren't a superior horsewoman I would have found you in the field an hour past, your obstinate little neck broken in several places," Pierre answered as another groom raced to the horse's head so that his master's son could dismount. "I know your limits, Caroline, perhaps better than you do yourself. I suggest you reflect on that for the remainder of the afternoon."

"I detest you!" she said, flinging the words at his departing back, causing the groom, who was about to walk Obtuse in order to cool him, to shake his head in silent condemnation.

"He's arrogant, insufferable, and entirely too sure of himself. I really, *really* detest that man," Caroline consoled herself repeatedly as she stalked back to the house, rhythmically slapping the riding crop against her thigh.

Perhaps if she repeated the words often enough she could make herself believe them.

"C'est bon pour les chiens; it is good for the dogs, and nothing else. *Mon Dieu,* how could this have happened?" Duvall was inconsolable. His master's best jacket was ruined past all repair, covered with horsehair and splashed with flecks of sticky, drying foam that had come from the mouth of the horse he had stretched to its limits during the search for that ungrateful Miss Addams. The valet held the offending jacket at arm's length in front of him by the tips of two fingers, his expression eloquent with disgust.

"First she arrives like a hair in the soup. That was the first sin, but not the last. We cannot escape from this terrible place to London because of her. The dirty little person is still with us because of her. But now, but now—this is the sideways of enough! Now she has caused for the so-beautiful jacket to be destroyed. I warn you, master, you won't buy another like this for a mouthful of bread."

Pierre, who had been listening to this tirade, and much more, from his valet all during his bath and while he was dressing for dinner, took one last look at himself in the mirror over his dressing table and was tolerably pleased with what he saw reflected there. "Your concern for my finances warms my heart, Duvall, even as your ceaseless chatter fatigues me. Kindly dispose of the thing. The smell of horse goes badly with the scent I have chosen for this evening."

Duvall was past caring whether or not he was displeasing his employer. After all, hadn't he, for two long hours only that morning, brushed this very coat into an absolute *merveille* of perfection? If his master had felt the need to go chasing after the so stupid Englishwoman, the least he could have done was think of his poor valet's dedicated efforts and changed his jacket before leaving. Where was the man's gratitude, his consideration? Duvall took one last, sorrowful look at the jacket, then dropped it out the open window onto the ground below, planning to fetch it later, in the hope he could at least rescue the silver buttons.

"And it has all gone for nothingness anyway," Duvall mused aloud. "She did not even have the decency to be killed. A fine jacket, ruined, and all for the wild geese chase. *C'est incroyable!*"

"Your logic never ceases to amaze me, Duvall," Pierre said, turning to his valet. "If Miss Addams had been murdered, then the sacrifice of my jacket would have been acceptable? Do you dislike women so much?"

"Appeler un chat un chat; to call a cat a cat, I say," Duvall responded reasonably. "A woman you can get anywhere, but a perfect jacket is not so easy to find."

Pierre's smile disappeared. "For the most part, my rationalizing friend, I agree with you. However, I value this particular woman a bit more than that. Someone is trying to kill Miss Addams, or at least make off with her. She was lucky today, if it can be called lucky to have had Oakvale for company, but at least his unlooked-for presence served to keep her safe from whoever is after her."

Taking his cue from his master, Duvall pushed all remaining regrets concerning the demise of the jacket from his mind and concentrated on the matter at hand. "The man in the gardens is then real?"

Pierre chose a ring from the tray on top of the dressing table and slipped it on the smallest finger of his left hand. "Someone did a good job of trampling down the shrubbery out there," he told the valet as he held his hand in front of him, considering the appropriateness of his choice of gold-encircled onyx over the plain gold ring he usually wore with this particular ensemble. "Not that I would tell Miss Addams that, of course. I see no good reason to alarm her. Unless, of course, she persists in trying to slip her leash." He turned to the valet, holding out his hand for that man's opinion. "What do you think, Duvall? Too much?"

Duvall, pleased that his employer had applied to him for guidance, immediately exploded into a torrent of complimentary French, extolling the man's utter perfection.

Monsieur's frame was exquisite, honoring the very fabric of which his ensemble had been constructed. The cravat, it was how you say, a triumph! The hair, so full, so thick with health, fit his head like a crown to a king. And the shoes! The shoes were—

"Fairly comfortable, thank you," Pierre broke in, moving toward the door. "Thank you, Duvall, for that rousing declaration. If you are correct, Miss Addams will swoon at the sight of me. That only leaves me with the question of whether I should welcome such an occurrence—or do my best to avoid it."

Duvall opened his mouth to give his opinion, but his master had shut the door behind him before he could voice it.

Pierre Standish excelled at polite yet interesting dinner table conversation, which was one of the many reasons he was welcomed everywhere in Mayfair, even if his hosts were never quite sure if their guest was laughing with them or at them.

He was also considered to be quite a success with the ladies, although he never seemed to exert himself to gain their good opinion. It was just that he was so very handsome, and so strangely mysterious, his dark good looks and incisive mind compelling all the young belles, and more than a few of their mothers, to try to discover the key to his locked heart. His massive fortune only added to the sweetness of the pie.

The masculine portion of society, whether they be titled lords, war heroes, or refined gentlemen of quality, were equally desirous of gaining Pierre's regard, but for the most part they were more than a little in awe of the man. He did not give of himself, did not engage in polite conversation or welcome confidences as much as he seemed to use some strange sixth sense to ferret out the motives and shortcomings of his fellow man.

While many prided themselves on being numbered among his acquaintance, and would have liked to know him better, only a few trusted friends were allowed into his inner circle. Partly this was due to Pierre's upbringing, and a father who had taught him that a man should consider himself blessed if he could number his real, true friends on the fingers of one hand. The unfortunate affair of Quennel Quinton's blackmail scheme had served to harden him, making him appear even more formidable than he was before serving in the Peninsula.

The women could not know that Pierre had been harboring an unfavorable opinion of the inconstancy of a female's affection, nor the men be aware that he had begun to look on all of mankind with a faintly jaundiced eye.

Caroline Addams, not knowing that she had been treated to a greater degree of friendliness by Pierre than almost every other female in England—thanks in part to André's admonition to find himself a redeeming charitable project—was also without knowledge of Pierre's reputation. She only knew that he was extremely handsome, curiously reticent, and maddeningly intriguing.

Like many of her sex, she wished she could somehow peel away the world-weary façade Pierre wore and get to know something of the real man that lay beneath the polished exterior. She wanted to see him react, whether in anger or passion she did not know. He was so cool, so controlled, so very perfect. His perfection, she had found, was the most annoying thing about him, and she longed to see him ruffled, on edge, unsure of himself.

"Human," she said aloud, walking into the drawing room a few minutes before the dinner gong was due to be rung. "That's what I want to see. Some sort of human emotion—and I don't count that dratted eyebrow as a display of anything other than disdain. I want to see him with his feathers ruffled, off his stride. And I want to be the one who causes his dishevelment."

"You said something, miss?"

Caroline whirled around, nearly tripping on the overly long hem of Eleanore Standish's gown. "Oh, Hartley, you startled me! I didn't see you over there. No, er, no, I didn't say anything. Did you think I said something? Oh, dear, I must have been talking to myself. I do that some-

times, don't you? Jeremy says it's a bad sign, and I might
end up part of the Sunday show in Bethlehem Hospital.
That would be too bad, wouldn't it?'' She laughed weakly
as the old retainer regarded her owlishly. ''Yes, ahem,
excuse me. I seem to be babbling. Did you want something, Hartley?''

Hartley shook his head while still looking at her
strangely, then bowed himself out of the room. ''There!''
Caroline groused, dropping heavily into a nearby chair.
''That is a fine example of what I'm talking about! Hartley
startled me, and I proceeded to make a cake of myself
trying to explain what I was doing. Pierre, on the other
hand, wouldn't have been overset in the least. He probably
would have turned, oh so slowly on his heels, lifted that
dratted eyebrow of his just so''—she tilted her chin upward and tried her best to imitate Pierre's haughty glance—
''and said, 'Ah, Hartley, you are here. How fortunate. If
it would not be too great an exertion on your part, might
I trouble you for a glass of port?' ''

''I make it a point never to drink port before a meal
myself, Caroline, as it ruins the palate. But, as Hartley
isn't here, might I play the part of loyal servant and fetch
you a small glass of sherry?''

For the second time in as many minutes, Caroline found
herself flying into nervous speech. ''Pierre! I didn't see
you there. Well, of course I didn't see you there, for you
weren't there, were you, or at least you weren't there a
moment ago. You are here now though, aren't you? Oh,
wasn't that the dinner gong? My, I'm starving. An afternoon on horseback will do that to one, won't it? Shall we
go in? It wouldn't do to have the meal cool, would it?''
She hated herself for what she was doing, and longed to
slap her hand over her mouth to stop the flow of words,
but she couldn't.

Only Pierre's left eyebrow, the one he was raising in
that oh-so-sophisticated way, could put a bridle on her
runaway tongue. That, and his next words: ''Caroline, far
be it from me to criticize, but you are babbling. Has Sir
John's company this afternoon so titillated you that you

are reduced to the simplest of chattering females? It would be such a pity, for I had thought you above such failings.''

Her eyes narrowed dangerously as she stood, intent on saying something so mean, so cutting, that he would flee the room in fear of her wrath. She glared at him while summoning something sufficiently nasty to say, her gaze raking him from his perfectly combed head to his brilliantly polished shoes. He looked, a part of her brain registered automatically, incredibly handsome in his ebony and white evening dress.

''Why must you always be so damnably perfect?'' she blurted without thinking of the consequences, suddenly feeling undersized and dowdy in her borrowed finery. ''Perfect speech, perfect clothes, perfect control—nobody should be so damnably perfect. Listen to me—I'm swearing like some fishwife! Oh! You make me so angry!''

Pierre didn't so much as blink, a lack of reaction that made Caroline mentally strike another black mark against him in the copybook she had begun keeping in her brain. ''Well? Aren't you going to say something?''

She watched as Pierre walked toward her, holding out his arm so that she might take it and together they could proceed to the dinner table. ''What would you like me to say, Caroline? You are obviously overwrought, and you are correct—it is entirely my fault. This perfection you speak of is my personal curse, but I did not mean to inflict it on you. Perhaps if I were to slurp during the soup course? Or would you rather I ate my peas with a knife? I should be willing to do anything to oblige you.''

She stopped, tugging on his arm so that his progress was halted as well. Looking up at him consideringly, she gave in to impulse and raised a hand, deliberately mussing the front of his hair so that it hung over his forehead. ''There,'' she said, standing back to admire her handiwork. ''That's more like it. You look almost human, Pierre. Now I believe I can do justice to my dinner.''

She took one step toward the dining room before Pierre's hand snaked out to grab her arm and pull her back. Without a word, he hauled her into his arms and kissed her, hard and long and quite thoroughly. When he released her, she was breathing heavily, her cheeks flushed a becoming pink and her lips softly swollen. "What—what did you do that for?" Caroline squeaked when at last she could speak.

Pierre studied his handiwork for a moment, gently running a fingertip across her slightly parted lips. "There," he said, smiling. "Now I *feel* human, and I, too, can enjoy my dinner."

Chapter Ten

It was a lovely country village lined with small thatched cottages, a pond at its center, and boasting not two but three perfectly wonderful little shops whose window displays captured Caroline's interest. So far she had purchased a wide yellow satin ribbon for her hair, a snow-white linen handkerchief with a delicate pink and green embroidered hem, a pair of tan leather riding gloves, and an ample supply of sugary hard candies, which she and her maid, Susan, were already sharing.

She disliked the idea that she had been reduced to spending Pierre Standish's money, but she was totally without funds of her own. She had fought and conquered her misgivings, knowing that, while there were a myriad of things she could continue to either borrow from Eleanore Standish's wardrobe or do without, there were also certain things she desperately needed.

The most important thing, the primary reason she had come to the village, was to purchase shoes that fit her. She was tired of retracing her steps to retrieve Eleanore's too-big slippers that kept falling off her feet. Of course, this didn't explain the purchases already lying in the basket Susan was carrying, but Caroline wasn't going to think about them now. She was just going to enjoy herself. She deserved it. She had earned every last copper penny of the money, too—having to endure Pierre Standish's insulting embrace.

Even now, the morning after her disgrace, her cheeks burned with embarrassment and indignation. And something more, something that she would rather not think about. For Caroline knew that most of her discomfort derived from the fact that she had enjoyed his kiss and had not fought to free herself from his arms.

For that, Pierre Standish would most certainly pay! She might just purchase a pair of riding boots. A very expensive pair of riding boots. She smiled wickedly. She might even kick him with them!

"Oh, look, Susan," she exclaimed, pulling the maid to a stop in front of a shop window. "There are just heaps and heaps of lovely shoes in here. Come along. I can't wait to get out of these uncomfortable slippers."

"Did you see that? She walked straight past us, just as if we weren't even here. Now do you believe me? She's dicked in the nob, just like I said."

A curiously pleased smile on her face, Amity Merrydell looked on as her quarry and the quarry's maid disappeared into the small shop. "I never said I didn't believe you, Ursley. Why must you malign me so? I told you—I have a plan."

Ursley sniffed derisively and leaned against the thin railing beside the street. "Some plan. We've been walking up and down this village day in and day out, with you all the time muttering about this great plan you have. All I see is that we are the ones who should be in that shop, for my boots are nearly worn through."

"Have you no faith in me? I knew she'd show up in the village sooner or later. It was too risky, trying to let her get a look at us at Standish's house. Now, come with me!" Grabbing her son by the elbow so that she could pull him into the small lane that ran beside the shop, Amity delivered a sharp slap to his cheek, just to be certain she had gained his undivided attention, then whispered: "Now listen to me and do precisely as I say."

"*Ow!* That hurt, Mama," Ursley whined, rubbing his stinging face. "You always do that. Why do you *always* do that."

Amity ignored him, leaning forward so that mother and

91

son were nose to nose. "We can't afford to bungle. Now, this is what you must do . . ."

Caroline was confused. There were so many pretty slippers and jean half boots, so many lovely colors and styles, that she couldn't make up her mind. Some she could have worn straight out of the shop, while some would take at least a week to be handcrafted to her measurements and then delivered. She would take the black slippers, of course, and perhaps the pink satin with the lovely grosgrain bows at the toe, but could she really decline a pair of white dancing slippers without regretting their absence?

"Oh, Susan," she said on a sigh, sitting back against the hard wooden chair to gaze down at her outstretched feet. "These are absolutely lovely. But I only have two feet, don't I? I really mustn't be greedy. Which do you prefer, the pink or the white?"

Susan, who had never owned more than two pair of shoes in her life—the ones on her feet and the ones she had just worn out—only shook her head. "It's perishin' difficult, miss, fer sure," she agreed, then spied the cobbler leaning over his counter to get a better look at Caroline's carelessly displayed shapely lower legs. "But, please, miss, lower yer skirts. Yer ankles are stickin' out for all the world and his wife to goggle at."

Caroline looked up to see the cobbler turning away, a sheepish expression on his face. "Sorry, Susan," she said, wondering yet again if she really was a lady of quality, for she seemed sadly prone to behaving like the worst sort of wayward creature. "I think I'll take these black ones and order the white ones. And the riding boots, of course. That goes without saying."

The door to the shop opened and a man entered, a young man dressed in what, considering the way he strutted into the place, he must have believed to be the height of fashion. He was not overly tall—not much taller than Caroline herself—and rather underfed, even hungry-looking, with a nose that could only be called unfortunate. His hair, once he had tipped his curly brimmed beaver jauntily in her direction and tucked it beneath his arm, was revealed to be mousy brown in color, and woefully sparse for a man so young. If Pierre Standish were to stand beside him, or even Sir John Oakvale, the man would escape notice, even if his hair suddenly caught fire.

Caroline quickly took all this in, then just as swiftly dismissed the gentleman from her mind and turned her attention back to her toes, wiggling them in pleasure as she realized that the slippers were a perfect fit.

"Good morning to you, you lovely creature," Ursley Merrydell drawled, making an elegant leg in front of Caroline. "I was just passing by this charming shop, out on the strut as it were, when I chanced to peep through the window and see you sitting here. As soon as I did my heart was smitten by your lovely face and form. Might I be so bold as to ask you to join me at the local inn for a repast—and possibly even greater pleasures?"

Caroline's jaw dropped a fraction as she stared up at the author of such an audacious speech. How dare he accost a gently reared female in this way? The man didn't look bosky. Or was it obvious that she *wasn't* what she hoped she was, and this strange man had instinctively recognized her as the sort of fast female who would welcome his less than innocent advances?

She was figuratively nailed to her chair by his words, and before she could think of a reply, Susan, who was standing behind Caroline, rushed into angry speech. "Away with yer now, yer filthy beast. This here lady's under Mr. André Standish's protection."

Ursley leered down at Caroline. "Standish's turtledove, are you? Well, from what I hear, he's away from home right now. And while the cat's away—" He didn't finish his sentence, only reached down to take hold of Caroline's upper arm and pulled her to her feet.

Caroline tried to shake him off, turning her head to yell to the cobbler, "Do something, for pity's sake!" just to have the cobbler retreat at once through the curtain at the back of his shop, leaving her alone with only Susan for protection. "Oh, that's just fine!" Caroline exploded, realizing that if she were going to be shed of this manhandling brute she would have to do it herself.

Her attacker now had both his hands on her, drawing her toward his descending mouth. "You'll get no order from me!" she yelled to the cowardly shopkeeper, twisting her head from side to side, trying to elude Ursley's lips. Why did she have to be so small? Even this skinny snake could hold her immobile with ease. Tears of frustration stung her eyes, which made her even angrier. "Let go of me, or I'll bite your ugly nose!" she warned impotently, for she could not move so much as an inch, his grip was so firm. Then, suddenly, her body went very still. Didn't she know this man? Hadn't they met somewhere before? No, it was impossible. If he knew her he would have immediately said something, would have called her by name.

Susan raced around the chair to begin whipping pieces of rock-hard candy straight at Ursley's head, screaming for him to "leave go, afore I brains yer!" while Caroline did her best to kick her attacker in the shins. It was unbelievable! She was being attacked right in the middle of the village, and in broad daylight.

The door to the shop slammed open and an older woman bounded through the door, her reticule already swinging above her head much the way David must have swung his slingshot as he prepared to slay Goliath. "Away with you, you nasty varlet!" she screamed at the top of her lungs, the reticule connecting with Ursley's head for at least a half dozen bruising blows. "Is there no safety for poor unguarded females in this terrible place!" With her free hand drawn into a tight fist, she then began beating against Ursley's back, causing him to stagger slightly and ease his hold on Caroline.

"Hey, not so hard!" he protested, turning to look at this new threat.

"If I were a man, I'd horsewhip you!" the lady warned fiercely, brandishing her reticule yet again. "I'm weary unto death with watching you young jackanapes assault unprotected females. A dozen years or more I've chaperoned young ladies of good birth and breeding, keeping them safe from the likes of you. Run along, varlet, or I'll have the constable on you!''

Ursley, who was feeling battered, threw the woman a foul look and made a break for the door, only to slip on one of Susan's pieces of candy ammunition, sense his feet sliding out from beneath him, and go crashing to the floor. His curly brimmed beaver, his most recent and therefore most prized possession, broke his fall, giving its life to save its owner. "Oh no, not my beaver!'' he exclaimed, sounding perilously close to tears.

By this time Caroline had recovered and was the next one to attack, picking up a nearby wooden clog that had obviously been fashioned to fit a very large foot and promptly tapping Ursley sharply atop his sparsely haired head. "Assault defenseless women, will you? Sit still, so I can hit you again!''

Scrambling on all fours, Ursley reached the doorway and quickly hauled himself up by grabbing on to the still open door. "Fie on you!'' he shouted dramatically, waving a fist in the air, his other hand clutching the worse-for-wear headgear. "I wouldn't have tried my evil wiles on you had I known you had a chaperone.''

A moment later he was gone, running down the flagway toward the safety of the inn, cursing his mother's heavy-handedness with the reticule and wishing he had not allowed himself to be a part of this charade.

Caroline, seated once more in her chair, fanned herself with her new handkerchief. "Where is your chaperone, miss, so that I might put a flea in her ear for leaving her charge unguarded?'' her rescuer asked, dabbing at her damp upper lip with the edge of her sleeve.

Caroline looked up at the tall, angular, rawboned woman who had so recently wielded her reticule like a regular Trojan, and smiled. "I have no chaperone, ma'am,'' she told her. "I am the ward of André Standish, but it is a male household. However, I should very much like to take you to meet Pierre Standish, who is in charge of me in his father's absence. I do believe he would like to deliver his thanks to you in person, for he is endlessly concerned for my well-being.''

Ignoring this invitation, the woman frowned, bringing her heavy black brows crashing together over the bridge of her nose. "No chaperone? It's unthinkable!" She fell silent, biting her bottom lip as if considering something known only to her. "Excuse me, miss, but are you happy without a proper chaperone, without some other gently raised female to bear you company and instruct you in how to go along? I am between positions now, having had my last charge married off quite successfully. If you would wish to engage my services, at least until your guardian can find a suitable chaperone of his own choosing, I should be happy to show you my references.''

It was Caroline's turn to frown. She hadn't really thought about it. Susan was her companion, of sorts, although she wasn't much of a conversationalist. Then again, Susan couldn't sit at the dinner table as a buffer between her and Pierre. She most certainly couldn't have saved her from Pierre's kiss last night in the drawing room.

A chaperone. Caroline smiled. What a splendid idea. A chaperone would go a long way toward putting a spoke in Pierre's wheels, wouldn't it? Rising, she held out her hands. "Excuse me for being so rude, but I do want to offer you my heartfelt thanks for saving me from that brute. My name is Caroline Addams, and you're—?''

"Caroline Addams? If you say—er, I'm Mrs. Merrydell, Mrs. Amity Merrydell,'' Amity offered quickly, taking Caroline's hand in her much larger one and shaking it heartily as a smile split her long, horsey face. "I know the way of it was unfortunate, Miss Addams, but I must say that it's a pleasure to meet you.''

Caroline tipped her head to one side, gazing up at the tall, rather formidable-looking woman whose strong grip was in danger of crushing her fingers. Pierre would dislike the slightly overwhelming woman on sight. Wasn't that just terrible? Caroline smiled, feeling very pleased with herself. She would do nicely. Oh, yes, Mrs. Amity Merrydell would do very nicely indeed. "Oh, on the contrary,

Mrs. Merrydell,'' she corrected sweetly, "I do believe that, in this case, the pleasure is entirely mine."

"I hate my mother," Ursley Merrydell muttered morosely, staring drunkenly at his battered hat as he sat in a corner of the common room at the small inn. "She's mean, and she's nasty, and she likes hitting me. She's a hateful, hateful woman."

He picked up his mug of ale, his fourth in less than an hour, and drained its contents in one long gulp. "Nasty woman," he said again, gingerly touching his fingertips to the side of his head, tracing the edges of the small lump that had been raised by something heavy in his mother's reticule. "Probably a rock she put in there, just for me. She's a nasty woman. Nasty, nasty, nasty."

She always had a plan, his mother did. Ursley had grown up listening to his mother's plans, the endless schemes she had concocted, designed to make them rich with only a minimum of effort. She and his father had once worked together, but that was all over now because his father had learned to love his gin too much and had bungled one too many of those neverending schemes.

"Poor Dada," Ursley said, his lower lip quivering as he considered his dead father, this time with sympathy for what must have been a wretched lifetime spent with Amity. "Why did I have to take after you? Why couldn't I have been big, like Mama? She hits so hard, Dada. I don't like it when she hits me. And after I was the one who figured out all about this losing her memory business in the first place. Mama wouldn't have had a plan at all if it weren't for me."

Ursley was seven and twenty, old enough by far to be on his own, if only he knew it, which he didn't. He had relied on his mother for all of his life, and it hadn't occurred to him to do things any other way. Most of the time she treated him very well, telling him how she loved him and buying him pretty things. It was only at moments like this, when she was hot on a plan, that she turned mean. And it was only at times like this, when Ursley was hurting, that a small, niggling thought having something to do with putting an ocean between himself and his battering mother appealed to him.

But there was all that lovely money to consider. He waved his hand halfheartedly at the barmaid, who plunked another heavy mug of ale in front of him, some of the dark, foamy liquid slopping over the top to splash on his hat. "Cow," he said, sneering as her generously rounded hips swished away from his table toward a group of men who had just come through the door. Ursley sneered not because he was angry but because he had earlier asked her to come up to his room after closing and she had laughed in his face.

Money. That's what he needed. The barmaid wouldn't laugh at him if he had gold to dangle in front of her greedy little face. Nobody would laugh then. And nobody would hit him, not ever again.

He lifted the mug and drank deeply. He'd go along with his mother's plan for now. He had seen her ride out of the village in the Standish carriage, and he acknowledged her plan certainly appeared to be working. If the rest went as well, they'd soon have more money than they'd ever dreamed of—lovely money, and a house all their own. Then his mother would take him to London for a Season, and he would marry a beautiful heiress who would bring them even more lovely money. It was a marvelous plan, a wonderful idea, and he still believed it, because it was a nice thing to believe.

But he wouldn't wait forever. If his abused head hadn't taught him anything else, it had taught him that he was all but through listening to Mama.

Chapter Eleven

Pierre paced the Aubusson carpet that covered the floor of his father's study, mentally ticking off the passing seconds on the mantel clock with each long, impatient stride and idly wondering if he was fast on his way to losing his senses.

Caroline had not been gone above two hours, surely not an unconscionable amount of time for a trip to the village and back, with space in there somewhere for whatever wildly expensive purchases she had decided upon as a perfect punishment for his unseemly advances last night before dinner. Besides, Susan was with her, as were his own coachman and a burly groom he had sent along for good measure. What could possibly happen to her?

Nothing could happen to her. He was overreacting, that was all, scratching around the barnyard like a hysterical old hen with but a single chick. He was taking this Good Deed thing beyond the bounds of common sense, and it was all his beloved father's fault. His beloved, *absent* father.

André's defection bothered Pierre, not because the man had gone to London, but because it had not occurred to Pierre that he would. He was slipping; he should have seen it coming. But Pierre, as his father had accused, had become overweeningly arrogant, and had forgotten that André had taught him everything he knew.

Obviously the teacher had thought it was time to give the student another lesson: never assume. Pierre knew he had *assumed* his father would react in a certain way and had proceeded to base his own actions on that assumption.

He should have known his father had always made it a point never to do the expected.

André was off somewhere, doing typical André things, which could mean anything from selecting just the sort of chaperone he would wish for Caroline, to discovering, in his own inimitable way, his ward's true identity.

"Both, probably," Pierre said aloud, shaking his head. "While reducing his son to the role of nursemaid." He stopped his interminable pacing for, besides making him look silly, the exercise was wearying, and he sank into a chair. This wasn't like him; it wasn't like him at all. He enjoyed being an observer, but a contributing observer, not just an impotent bystander relegated to a minor role.

He could have hired a man, a dozen men, to ensure Caroline's safety. That was elementary. Discovering who she was, who was intent on harming her, and why—those were important things.

"Obviously too important to entrust to a mere son," Pierre remarked to the empty room. "I do believe I am insulted. Now, what in blazes was that?"

He had heard the sound of something breakable hitting the tiled foyer floor, followed by a deep, masculine shout. Pierre only had time to turn his head toward the sound before the door crashed open, banging loudly against the wall, and Jeremy charged into the room, looking back over his shoulder as if the hounds of hell were after him.

"Yer'll not git yer maggoty mitts on me agin, yer beetle-browed bogey!" he shouted as he ran. "Oi'm not goin' nowheres with the likes of yer!"

Pierre stood up in time to catch Jeremy by the shoulders, effectively halting him in his tracks. "I assume there's some reasonable explanation for this interruption, my young friend?" he asked, looking over Jeremy's head to the hallway. "There are, after all, more elegant ways of entering a room."

Jeremy looked up at Pierre, his eyes wide with fright even as a new determination squared his jaw. " 'E's not gonna snaffle me, is 'e, guv'nor? Yer said yer wuz gonna take me ter Piccadilly. Yer can't lets 'im take me."

"I don't recall expressing any wish to be shed of you," Pierre responded, "although I must admit that the lapse amazes even me." He released Jeremy's shoulders, only to have the boy fall to the carpet and wrap his arms convulsively around Pierre's knees. "I think it only fair to warn you, brat, that I am known to dislike dramatic displays," he added, looking down at Jeremy's fuzzy yellow head.

"There yer be, yer dirty, snivelin' heathen!"

Pierre looked up to see that there was now a very large, very dirty man standing on his father's lovely Aubusson carpet. He pointed out as much to the man. "You're standing on my father's Aubusson carpet, my good fellow," he said, his voice smooth as finest velvet. "My gratitude would know no bounds if you would remove your boots from it at once."

The man halted in his tracks, looked about as if wondering how he had happened to enter the elegant room, then backed up until his boots were once more touching polished wood, two feet away from the carpet.

"I do so admire obedience," Pierre complimented, nodding in the man's direction. "I don't believe we've been introduced. Master Holloway—as you appear to have the advantage of knowing the name of our unexpected visitor—would you be so kind as to do the honors?"

Jeremy spoke from the presumed safety of his position, still at Pierre's feet. He was safe now, he was sure, as the "guv'nor" was all powerful and would let no harm come to him. "Dat's 'im, the sweep. Dat's ol' 'Awkins. 'E's come ter do yer da's chimleys an' spotted me. Slit 'is slimy gizzard, guv'nor! Chop up 'is liver an' lights an' feed 'em ter the crows!"

"So bloodthirsty, Master Holloway. I cannot fathom why you and Duvall do not hit it off. You have so much in common." Pierre's left eyebrow lifted fractionally as he turned his attention back to the man. "So, you're Mr. Hawkins?" he remarked silkily. "This young lad has mentioned you more than once, as you've made a strong impression on him—most frequently with a fireplace poker, as I recall. I must say I'm surprised. My compliments to

101

you. I hadn't thought a creature such as you could actually walk upright."

The sweep master's huge hands bunched into tight fists, and he took two steps forward, his boots once again on the carpet.

"Tut-tut!" Pierre admonished pleasantly. "The carpet, sir, if you'll recall."

Hawkins backed up, although if anyone had asked him why he had done so he would have been hard-pressed to explain. The gentry mort hadn't been born that could scare Jacky Hawkins. There was just something about this particular one that had made him consider a small retreat preferable to whatever unspoken alternative Pierre Standish might have in mind. His voice rose, to cover his sudden attack of cowardliness. "Dat there boy belongs ter me," he whined, pointing a grimy finger at Jeremy. "Oi paid fer him right an' tight. Oi don't want no trouble, guv'nor. Oi only wants wot's mine."

Pierre appeared to be unmoved by Hawkins's logic. "Master Holloway," he questioned softly, "much as I have recently developed a most prodigious aversion to assumption, may I assume that you do not wish to reenter Mr. Hawkins's employ?"

"Oi'd druther 'ave a bleedin' stick stuffed up m' nose!" Jeremy lifted his head to demonstrate, with the use of his index finger. "Jist like this!"

Pierre shuddered delicately. "There you have it, Mr. Hawkins, straight from the boy's, er, mouth. Now, if you'll excuse us, I believe this young man and I have wearied of this conversation. Please be so good as to close the door behind you as you leave the room and, I believe, this house. Your services are no longer required."

Hawkins slammed his hamlike fists against his hips as his face turned a violent purple. "Oi ain't steppin' one foot nowheres till Oi 'ave that kiddy back right an' tight. 'E's mine, Oi says."

"Yes, you did say, Mr. Hawkins," Pierre said consideringly. "How fatiguing it is to listen to it a second time, for it now becomes my sad chore to repeat myself by again requesting your immediate departure.''

Hawkins knew he could break Pierre Standish in half, just as if he were a dry stick. He was twice his size, wasn't he, and no stranger to fighting. So why was he standing there like a stuffed bear, doing nothing? Why, indeed? He took one step onto the carpet.

Pierre's left eyebrow rose the merest fraction.

''Oi'm out good blunt for that worthless brat!'' Hawkins shouted, shaking his fist at Jeremy. But for all his bellowing, he didn't bring his second foot forward.

''Are you suggesting that I reimburse you, Mr. Hawkins?'' Pierre smiled, and Hawkins shivered. ''I'm afraid I shall have to disappoint you there, as I do not traffic in human souls, either in the buying or the selling of them.''

''Oi'll have the law on yer! Yer nuthin' but a thievin' low-down bastard!''

''Oh, dear, really?'' Pierre leaned down to touch Jeremy's shoulder. ''Excuse me, Master Holloway, but I must implore you to remove your arms, as I believe your convulsive grip has served to put my feet to sleep. Ah, thank you, that's much better.'' He stepped away from the child without moving closer to Hawkins.

''Don't leave me, guv'nor!'' Jeremy screeched, panic-stricken at this seeming desertion by the one man he had grown to trust. ''Wot are yer gonna do now?''

Pierre turned back to the boy, smiling widely. ''Do, Master Holloway? Why, I would have thought you'd know. I'm going to challenge our Mr. Hawkins to a duel, as any gentleman must do when his honesty and honor have been impugned. First I will slap him, with a glove or handkerchief of course, as I would not wish to soil my hand, and then I shall ask Mr. Hawkins to name his weapon of choice. I favor pistols, or even swords, but as I have not had the chance for more than a few rounds with Gentleman Jackson in these past months, fisticuffs would appeal to me as well. What say you, Mr. Hawkins?''

Pierre looked to where Hawkins had been standing a

moment earlier, to see that the room was now empty of anyone save Jeremy and himself.

"How odd," he remarked, shaking his head. "It would appear, Master Holloway, that your Mr. Hawkins has undergone a change of heart. Pity. A duel would have filled an hour nicely."

Jeremy hopped to his feet, punching the air as he danced about the room in imitation of some bruiser he had once seen perform an impromptu demonstration of the manly science of fisticuffs on a street corner. "Yer woulda kilt 'im, guv'nor," he assured Pierre. "Yer woulda shoved yer fives right square in 'is ivories, so dat 'is daylights popped out. It'd 'ave been grand ter see ol' 'Awkins arsy varsey, 'is applecart spilled, guv'nor. Real grand! Wot a sight fer sore eyes it'd 'ave been!"

"Please remember that a gentleman is never vulgar in victory, Master Holloway, any more than he is ungracious in defeat," Pierre admonished, patting the boy on the head. "Now run off and see if you can be of some help in the kitchens. Or you might wish for me to ring for Duvall, so that you might have another bath?"

Jeremy ran from the room as fast as his legs would carry him, and Pierre settled once more into a chair, looking toward the mantel clock and wondering where the devil Caroline could be, the incident with Hawkins, which had been at best only a small diversion, already forgotten.

It never occurred to him, that, had Caroline seen his protection of Jeremy, her low opinion of him would have undergone a considerable change for the better.

The nearer the carriage carried her to Standish Court the more apprehensive Caroline became about her impetuous decision to employ Mrs. Merrydell.

The woman was not at all what she would have had in mind for a chaperone, if indeed she had ever considered the requirements for such a person.

Her references, which the woman had produced from the single piece of luggage that the coachman had picked up from the local inn and insisted Caroline read as they rode along in the carriage, were impeccable; three letters, all signed by titled ladies whose penmanship was only slightly superior to their imaginative spelling.

It was the woman herself who bothered Caroline. She was loud, for one thing, and rather coarse, and had a disconcerting habit of nudging Caroline none too gently in the ribs to emphasize her stories of how she had contrived to successfully "pop off" many an eligible young miss in her time.

Knowing that her own language could at times stray embarrassingly close to the barracks, Caroline tried hard to overcome her objections to Mrs. Merrydell's speech, but there was a world of difference between a good swearword when it fit the situation and talking openly about such things as "firm little titties" when the woman described the physical attributes of her last charge.

What had begun as a ploy to infuriate Pierre Standish had rapidly descended into a ticklish situation that was, among other things, fast giving Caroline the headache. Even Susan, who was for the most part a placid sort, was showing signs of wishing to stuff something in Mrs. Merrydell's mouth in order to shut her up.

As the carriage stopped in front of the main entrance to Standish Court, Caroline soothed herself with the thought that Pierre would have Mrs. Merrydell's measure in less than a heartbeat, and would immediately show her the door, if only to thwart his unloved Good Deed. He would instinctively know that she had engaged the woman only to inconvenience him and would refuse to allow her to remain as chaperone.

She smiled as the groom lowered the steps and held out his hand to help her down. Pierre would take care of everything. For once she was glad for his interference in her life.

Leading the way, Caroline swept across the foyer after learning Pierre's whereabouts from the footman, ignoring something he tried to tell her about a rare goings-on just having taken place, and knocked at André's study door. "Come along, Mrs. Merrydell, and meet your new employer," she urged as that woman hesitated a moment, assessing a large vase that stood in a corner of the foyer as if considering what price it would bring on the open market.

When no one called for her to enter, Caroline knocked a second time, then opened the door.

"Ah, Miss Addams," Pierre drawled, rising languidly from his chair. "Please forgive me for not begging you to enter, but I was enjoying the notion that there are still people in this world who ask permission to enter a room. You've concluded your visit to the village?"

Caroline stood in the doorway, not understanding what he was referring to and suddenly reluctant to enter. He seemed inordinately happy, and that disturbed her. "I have," she answered shortly.

"And now you've come to show me your purchases. How gratifying. Please, don't hover in the doorway. Come in, and let me see what you've got. There wouldn't be a surprise for me, would there?"

She tipped her head to one side, as if considering the question. "Wel-l-l, *actually,*" she began, sliding her hands behind her back and crossing her fingers for luck, "there is one little surprise."

"Really? I am, of course, breathless to learn more," Pierre told her, advancing across the room. "Now what, I must ask myself, would Miss Addams consider to be a suitable gift for me?"

"Ooooff!" Caroline felt a none-too-gentle poke in the back and staggered three full steps into the room.

"Enough of this shilly-shallying!" Mrs. Merrydell protested, pushing past Caroline to confront Pierre. "This here gel was being attacked in the village, no thanks to you, until I came to her rescue. No chaperone," she said, shaking her head. "It's shameful, that's what it is. But that's all over now, for Amity Merrydell is here. Are you the one who is in charge? You look mighty young to me. There isn't anything havey-cavey going on, is there? I'm a good woman, and I won't be a party to any shifty dealings."

Pierre, staring past Mrs. Merrydell to Caroline, blinked once, then waited for his Good Deed to speak.

"I—she—that is, I—hired her," Caroline gulped out, wondering if that bump on her head had proved to shake out her common sense as well as her memory. She must be the victim of a temporary mental aberration! How else could she explain Mrs. Merrydell?

Pierre nodded. "You hired her," he repeated, his voice calm. "I see."

And he did see. He saw everything. That was what was so maddening. He always saw everything, drat him anyway. Caroline longed to fly at him and shake him into reacting. "A strange man made advances toward me while I was being fitted for some shoes—lovely shoes, in white, and a black pair, and some riding boots as well, but that's nothing to the point now, is it?—and Mrs. Merrydell rescued me and, and I hired her as my chaperone." He'd done it again—he had her babbling like the village idiot!

"How very enterprising of you," Pierre said coolly, but he was looking at Mrs. Merrydell as he said it. "Please excuse me—Mrs. Merrydell, I believe you said? You must think I am the rudest beast in nature. Won't you ladies be seated while I ring for some refreshments. You must both still be terribly overset. Only then will I prevail upon you for details of what must have been a truly terrifying ordeal."

"That's it?" Caroline asked incredulously, unable and unwilling to believe Pierre was taking her news so well. "That's all you have to say?"

He tugged on the bell rope, then turned to look at her inquiringly. "What else is there to say? I should have liked to have been there, to protect you, but we were fortunate enough to have found a protector in the so estimable Mrs. Merrydell, who immediately took you under her wing. You seem to have no end of protectors, Miss Addams, which is fortunate for you, as you seem to have an inordinate need for protection.

"Mrs. Merrydell?" he said, looking toward the woman now seated comfortably in his father's chair. "Do you by chance play the harp? My father and I would so enjoy it if you could instruct Miss Addams in its use. Oh dear, I can see by your expression that you do not. A pity, but there it is. Doubtless you have many other skills. Ah, Hartley, there you are, prompt as usual. Would you be so kind as to procure some refreshments for the ladies? Ladies, just tell Hartley every little thing you require.''

Caroline stomped across the room to stand toe-to-toe with Pierre. "I don't *require* anything, you dolt," she hissed at him from behind clenched teeth. "Why are you doing this? You know full well Mrs. Merrydell is completely unacceptable. I only brought her to upset you. For God's sake—*get rid of her!*"

Pierre waved a hand at Mrs. Merrydell, who was busily ordering a meal fit for a smithy who had just completed twelve full hours at his forge, and drawled urbanely, "Why, Caroline, my dear, whatever do you mean? I think Mrs. Merrydell is an admirable choice for a chaperone. Sturdy, firm-minded, and not about to take any nonsense. Just what I would have wished for you myself."

"I *despise* you," Caroline whispered harshly, knowing that he had bested her once again.

Pierre lifted her chin with one long finger and smiled down into her face. "No, darling girl, you don't. Why that pleases me I am not sure, but I am confident I will work it out in time. Now, be a good little charge and go have some tea. I just remembered that I have somehow promised Master Holloway a chess lesson this afternoon."

Caroline was staring at him, unable to move. "A—a chess lesson?" she asked, incredulous.

"Yes," he answered, letting go of her chin. "My kindness astonishes even me. Ladies, your most obedient," he said, bowing elegantly before leaving Caroline alone in the room with a grinning Mrs. Merrydell.

Chapter Twelve

The doctor leaned over Caroline as he examined the bump on her head. "Ah, good, very good. The swelling has gone down quite nicely, Miss Addams, as I'm sure you are already aware. Physically, I would say you have completely recovered, which is no great surprise for, as I told Mr. Standish after the first examination, you are young and healthy."

"Young, healthy, and *anonymous*, Doctor Burgess," Caroline pointed out.

The doctor frowned his concern. "You've remembered nothing?"

Glad his examination was over, she patted her hair back in place, "Mere snatches, Doctor Burgess. Nothing that means anything."

"Snatches? You've remembered snatches? What sort of snatches?" Mrs. Merrydell, who had been sitting at her ease in a corner of the bedchamber, hastily hopped to her feet to approach her charge in what could only be termed a challenging manner. "Naughty, secretive girl. You only said you had lost your memory in an accident. You told me nothing of snatches!"

Caroline, who had wearied of Mrs. Merrydell's constant company within minutes of meeting her and who had—thanks to that perverse Pierre Standish—had to endure the crude woman from morning to night for three full days, ignored this latest outburst and directed her reply to the doctor. "I know that I can ride, paint, and dance. Nothing more. Nothing even remotely personal."

"I see," said Doctor Burgess, frowning down on her from overtop his spectacles.

"Wonderful!" exclaimed Mrs. Merrydell, adding quickly, "That is to say, it's a start, my dear, a start. You shouldn't force yourself to remember—should she, Doctor? I mean, it might be injurious—to her spleen, or something."

Doctor Burgess who, if truth be told, had no real knowledge of Caroline's particular complaint outside of the meager bits he had gleaned from one of his medical books, hastily agreed with the woman. "That goes without saying, Mrs. Merrydell. We wouldn't wish to fall victim to a brain fever, would we?"

Caroline looked back and forth between the two faces hovering above her and shook her head. "No, I imagine *we* wouldn't. But what if I never remember who I am? I can't spend the remainder of my life not knowing my own name. I would surely go insane."

"Oh, but we can't count on—that is, we shouldn't even *think* of such a terrible thing! Most assuredly not!" Mrs. Merrydell protested, grabbing Caroline's two hands and squeezing them convulsively. "You will just have to take each day as it comes, my dear. Isn't that the ticket, Doctor?"

Doctor Burgess was beginning to tire of his role as acquiescent bystander and walked to the side table to retrieve his bag. He snapped it closed with some force. The Merrydell woman wasn't a doctor, after all. It was time he took charge of the situation. "I begin to think Miss Addams must have some terrible secret locked inside her memory, some awful event that has made it preferable for her to forget everything that has happened to her. This might be the time to call in the local constable. Perhaps he can shed some light on the situation."

"The constable!" Caroline and Mrs. Merrydell cried in unison.

Now the center of attention, Doctor Burgess nodded thoughtfully. "The constable," he repeated solemnly. "If there has been any terrible accident in the neighborhood

110

he would know of it, as well as whether or not a young lady of Miss Addams's description has gone missing. Yes, I think that is a sterling idea. I wonder why Mr. Standish hasn't thought of it himself.''

"Ah, good doctor, but he has."

Three heads turned to see Pierre Standish standing in the doorway, his arms folded across his chest. "Pierre!" Caroline cried, hopping down from the bed to approach him. "You spoke with the constable about me?" She couldn't decide if she should be glad that he had exerted himself for her or angry that he had thought she was notorious enough to be known to the local constable.

Taking her elbow so that he could lead her to a nearby chair, Pierre answered, "Not I, actually, but my father. He ordered a thorough inquiry to be launched throughout the district, but to no avail. So sorry to disappoint you, Doctor, but that is neither here nor there, is it? How is our patient? Will she live?"

Doctor Burgess cleared his throat and puffed out his chest, clearly taking full credit for what he told Pierre was Miss Addams's astonishing recovery from a terrible blow to the head. "There is no reason for me to attend her again, unless you wish me to, of course. There is really nothing else I can do for her at this time."

Mrs. Merrydell was quick to agree, pointing out that she was in charge now and perfectly capable of supervising Miss Addams's welfare. "She's in no danger while *I'm* about!" she ended determinedly.

"Danger, Miss Merrydell?" Pierre repeated, his smooth voice tinged with surprise. "Whoever said Miss Addams was in any danger? Surely I haven't spoken of danger. We were speaking only of unfortunate accidents, I believe."

Taking refuge in righteous anger, Mrs. Merrydell placed her hands on her hips and challenged hotly, "And just who was it who saved her from that cheeky dandy in the village, Mr. Standish? There is no end of danger to a well-bred young woman left to fend for herself. Heaven only knows what trouble she could have gotten herself into if *I* hadn't been there to save her."

Caroline shook her head slowly as she rose to cross to the bed, wearied to death by Mrs. Merrydell's constant repetition of her bravery in rescuing her at the shoemaker's. "I think I should like to lie down for a while, if you don't mind," she said in a voice all but dripping with maidenly fatigue, hoping everyone would take her hint and withdraw so that she might have a moment's peace. "We can regroup at luncheon to hear, while eating our stuffed capon, Mrs. Merrydell's hundredth reenactment of her daring rescue."

"Well! That's gratitude for you," Mrs. Merrydell said, sniffing. "Not that I'm not used to it, as a chaperone often feels she has taken a viper to her bosom," she added as she headed for the hallway. "Doctor Burgess, please allow me to show you the door."

Caroline stretched out on the satin coverlet, closing her weary eyes. Her headache, which had abated within hours of her awakening after the accident, had returned at almost the exact moment Mrs. Merrydell had entered her life, the constant dull ache behind her eyes showing every indication of becoming a permanent part of her. She would do anything—anything—to be shed of the woman.

"Another headache, Caroline?" Pierre questioned solicitously, startling her, for his voice came from directly beside the bed. "I wouldn't want to think you were going into a sad decline. Father would be so angry with me. Is there anything I can do?"

Without opening her eyes, she suggested dully, "You could have dear, sweet Mrs. Amity Merrydell bound and gagged and set on a freighter heading for the West Indies at dawn. That would go a long way toward alleviating my pain."

"No," he answered, chuckling softly at her show of vehemence. "As much as I regret it, I cannot do that. I still have need of the woman."

Caroline's eyes popped open and she glared at him. "Whatever for? Or have you not yet wearied of your latest revenge on me? I admit it, the woman was a mistake. I only brought her here to get some of my own back on you.

I never thought you'd open your father's house to her."
Her eyes narrowed as a sudden thought hit her. "What do
you know that I don't know?"

Pierre reached down to stroke a finger along Caroline's
jaw. "Almost everything, infant, almost everything. Have
a nice nap and we'll take this up later, as I'm sure you
will not be satisfied until you have asked me at least a
dozen new questions, for which, I regret, I as yet have no
answers."

As Caroline suspected, luncheon with Pierre and Mrs.
Merrydell did not shed any new light on either her identity
or Pierre's reasons for allowing Mrs. Merrydell to continue to run tame in his father's household. In fact, other
than to ask some probing questions concerning her chaperone's last few employment situations, Pierre kept the
conversation very light and very general. All in all, if it
wasn't for cook's disarming way with capons, the meal
would have been a total waste of Caroline's time.

Hoping that putting some fresh air and distance between
herself and her resident dragon would serve to clear her
head, Caroline changed into her riding habit immediately
after luncheon and departed for the stables. The first person she met there was Jeremy, whom, she realized, she
hadn't seen in several days.

"How are you going on, Jeremy?" she asked conversa-
tionally while waiting for the groom to saddle Lady, the
mare Pierre had set aside for her personal use. Lady was
a far cry from Obtuse, but she was spirited enough, and
Caroline had already grown to love her gentle ways.

"Oi'm learnin' ter be a groom, missy," he told her
proudly, standing tall. "Oi doesn't like it much bein' inside, so guv'nor 'as me workin' 'ere. Oi've all but decided
not ter go back ta Piccadilly. Did yer 'ear 'ow guv'nor set
ol' 'Awkins ter the rightabout? It waz a rare sight ter see,
Oi tells yer, a rare sight!"

"Guv—er, Mr. Standish routed your former master?"
she asked, sorting through Jeremy's heavily accented
slang. "I knew a sweep was coming, of course, but I

never thought it could have been *your* sweep. Oh, this is delicious. Tell me about it.''

As she urged Lady into a canter that would not outdistance the groom Pierre had assigned to her, Caroline considered all that Jeremy had told her. Even leaving off some of the lad's sure to be broad exaggerations, Pierre had done a wonderful thing, a wonderfully unselfish thing, by defending the little sweep. ''And it was totally out of character,'' she mused aloud. ''I will never understand the man. Not that I wish to,'' she added hastily, the memory of Pierre's kiss once again entering her mind unbidden.

Pierre was a puzzle she was not ready to solve, for her own puzzle, the one of her true identity, must necessarily take first place of importance in her mind. All her energies must be—had to be—directed toward learning who she really was. The doctor's words returned to her, making her wonder if she could have been involved in some sort of carriage accident, hitting her head and then wandering off, only to faint in the roadway where Pierre had first seen her.

It seemed a logical explanation, but if there had been an accident surely André Standish's inquiries would have discovered the event. No, there had to be another reason for what had happened to her.

She continued to ride Lady across the open fields, the breeze lifting her dark curls and putting an attractive blush on her cheeks. She thought about the cloak she had been wearing, the man's cloak she had examined without a hint of recognition. Where had the cloak come from? Who had it belonged to? Why had she been wearing it, instead of some cloak of her own?

''And I was barefoot,'' she said aloud, Lady's pointed ears flicking alertly at the sound of her mistress's voice. ''How far could I have gone on foot without shoes? Not any great distance, surely. After all, my feet were barely bruised.''

Out of the corner of her eyes she saw a lone horseman approaching, and shivered in sudden panic, only to relax when she recognized the handsome, vacant face of Sir

John Oakvale. She smiled as he waved gaily and "yoo-hooed" her, silently admonishing herself for becoming so skittish over the doctor's speculative prattling and Mrs. Merrydell's melodramatic ramblings about danger. She was in no danger; the idea was ridiculous! Of course, there had been that man in the gardens, she reminded herself fleetingly, but the incident had come to nothing. Determinedly widening her smile, she banished her dark thoughts.

"Good afternoon to you, Miss Addams," Sir John said, pulling his mount up beside Lady so that the horses could walk together. "I was hoping to pay a call on you before this, but m' father's been ill, you understand, so I've had to curtail my social activities for a time."

"Oh, dear. Nothing serious, I hope," Caroline returned politely.

Sir John shook his head. "No, just a small tea party with the aunts and, of course, the dance over at the squire's. I really didn't miss anything of importance."

Caroline barely suppressed a giggle. "I meant your *father,* Sir John."

"You did? Of course you did!" he exclaimed, hooting with laughter. "How silly of me. Just a touch of the gout, though it makes him growl like a bear with a sore paw. How are you going along with Pierre Standish now that his father has flown the coop? Not that you haven't got yourself a real dragon of a chaperone."

Caroline's head snapped slightly back. "Gossip, Sir John?" she admonished regally. "I would have thought gentlemen to be above such things. Have I become a topic of conversation in the neighborhood?"

Sir John cast a wary glance behind him at the groom who was riding in their wake. "No, no! Of course not! Dear me, I wouldn't think of it. It's just that it's so dashed dull in the country, you understand. A nameless young lady is just the thing to set all the biddies to tittering behind their fans. Jealous, too, I imagine, seeing as how you've captured the elusive Pierre Standish for your very own."

Caroline bristled. "I have not *captured* anyone, and do not care to do so. It's the furthest thing from my mind. You will make that perfectly clear to the ladies, won't you, Sir John?"

Sir John nodded furiously, knowing he had gone too far. "Oh, look, there's that stand of trees we visited upon our first meeting. I think my mount can outrun your mare. Shall we race, Miss Adams?"

Angry that she had allowed herself to be flustered by Sir John's mention of Pierre, Caroline immediately took up the challenge and, before the groom could utter a word of censure, the two spurred their mounts into a gallop. Sir John's mount, a showy but heavy-rumped grey, was no match for Lady, and soon Caroline was two lengths ahead of him, turning her head to laugh back at his rapidly diminishing figure.

Without warning, the sidesaddle began to shift beneath her, and she had to turn her full attention to controlling Lady, who momentarily misplaced her gentle disposition at this startling development. Hauling on the reins with more force than delicacy, for her entire body was now shifting dangerously toward the ground, Caroline clenched her teeth and held on for all she was worth.

With a sickening lurch, the girth slipped completely sideways and Caroline, her foot still in the stirrups, was flung backwards onto the ground and dragged along the surface of the field, pulled by one caught leg.

Lady's hooves flashed dangerously close to her head as clumps of dirt and sharp stones bit into her back. There was no chance to wonder how the girth had loosened, or why. She felt no pain, for there wasn't time for such an indulgence; she only knew she had to free her foot before she was either trampled or dragged to her death.

How she did it she would never know, but she raised a hand to grab convulsively onto part of the saddle and levered herself upward until she could swing her booted foot free of the stirrup. Within a heartbeat she crashed back toward the ground, only to roll over and over in the dirt until her soft body was rudely introduced to an unfortunately placed boulder that put a sudden halt to her progress.

A moment later Sir John was by her side, holding her limp hand in his and moaning, "My God, Miss Addams, please, please don't be dead. If you're dead Standish will kill me!"

Pierre paced the sunlit drawing room, idly wondering if he should send word to the stables to have Obtuse saddled so that he could join Caroline on her ride. He could stand the exercise, he knew, for he felt like a caged lion trapped within doors on such a fine day, but still he didn't pull the bell rope and give the order.

It would be entirely too dangerous, being alone with Caroline, with none but the birds and the horses to act as chaperones. He was too attracted to her, and she was too attracted to him.

He smiled at this last thought. Yes, Caroline Addams was attracted to him, even if she would rather die than admit it. This attraction was a comforting yet unsettling thought. Certainly he hadn't encouraged her; quite the opposite. But it was true nevertheless, and he was secretly pleased.

It was also an impossible situation. He was years older than she, for one thing, not that anyone put much stock in such things. More important was that no one knew just who Caroline really was. She was a lady, of that he was sure; a very young, very beautiful lady of quality. But was she titled? Was she married? Was she eligible or ineligible?

And what was she eligible for? he asked himself, still pacing the carpet for all he was worth. Surely his mind wasn't running toward thoughts of matrimony? The notion was ludicrous. He, Pierre Claghorn Standish, in the role of doting bridegroom? It was past imagining.

But there was the kiss to consider, that one brief interlude when he had held her in his arms. Her touch had brought with it a startling revelation. He was vulnerable to a woman's charms—to a certain woman's charms.

Perhaps she reminded him of his mother, dressed in his mother's gowns as she was. But no. He wasn't that uncomplicated, or that gullible. It was Caroline herself who intrigued him; the Caroline whose astonishingly beautiful eyes were the unknowing mirror of her soul; the Caroline who spat fire and passion and clear, insightful intelligence; the Caroline who championed a young chimney sweep and had no idea what to do with a mouthful of unwanted kippers.

Oh, he was definitely in serious trouble, Pierre decided, shaking his head in a fine imitation of self-pity. How André would crow if he could but see him now. There was nothing else for it—he would have to ferret out her true identity as soon as possible and then put half a country between them. Perhaps an ocean wouldn't be far enough.

"Master Pierre?" Hartley's voice came from a doorway, interrupting Pierre's disquieting train of thought. "There's a lady here to see you, sir. I told her I'd ask if you're receiving today."

"A lady?" Pierre mused almost to himself. "This is unexpected. Does the plot perhaps begin to thicken?" More loudly he bade Hartley to show the lady in at once, and a few moments later a handsome young woman dressed in fashionable traveling clothes sailed through the door. "Victoria!" he exclaimed in real delight, holding out both hands to his visitor. "I don't believe it. Is Patrick with you? Surely he hasn't let you out of his sight already?"

Victoria Quinton Sherbourne, now Countess Wickford, was definitely in looks this day, her soft, rose-colored gown giving a decided bloom to her cheeks, the sparkle in her intelligent eyes and the enchanting dimple in her left cheek making it possible for the people she met to forget that she was not a classically beautiful woman. Her appearance was a far cry from the too-thin, drab, sad creature Pierre had first seen in Quennel Quinton's library the day that unlovely man's will had been read. It was remarkable how being loved, and in love, could bring such marvelous changes in a person.

After allowing Pierre to kiss her on the cheek—a display of affection he had never employed with her before—she stood back, used the index finger of her left hand to push her spectacles more firmly onto her nose, and said wonderingly. "Good Lord, Pierre, your father was correct. You *have* mellowed. I never would have believed it. Patrick will be devastated to have missed it. I must meet the young lady at once and offer her my congratulations."

Chapter Thirteen

"And so," Victoria concluded as she sat at her ease on one of the satin settees in the drawing room a few minutes later, gracefully pouring tea into a bone china cup, "no matter how great the inducement—and I must tell you that your father has quite a way with explanation, revealing just enough to pique an overwhelming interest and not a jot more—there was just no possible way for Patrick to abandon his project at such a crucial point and join me on this terribly unsubtle, curiosity-satisfying expedition."

"Expedition?" Pierre cut in, waving away her offer of tea and hot buttered scones in favor of a slightly stronger liquid refreshment. "Does dearest Patrick believe I am a mountain to be climbed? I assure you, I am the most uncomplicated of men, with nothing to hide."

"Perhaps expedition is too harsh a term for it. Let's just call it a friendly visit," Victoria corrected, obviously aware she had somehow struck a nerve and deciding to twist the knife a bit, in a friendly way, of course. "It goes without saying that Patrick sends his most profound regrets, as well as his equally profound professions of anguish at not being privileged to see you, his unflappable friend, at sixes and sevens."

She set down her teacup and leaned forward expectantly. "You are at sixes and sevens, aren't you, Pierre? I cannot tell you how depressing it would be to find that you are still your usual self, infuriatingly secretive and most maddeningly heart-whole."

"My father has painted you a melodramatic picture of

his only son as a brokenhearted swain, perhaps even entertaining thoughts of suicide? I must remember to be kinder to him in future, as it is evident he is fast entering his dotage.''

"Oh? Then you deny being interested in the poor, nameless girl whom you brought to your father's house to recover from some accident?'' Victoria countered, peering intently at him overtop her spectacles. "When Patrick questioned your father as to your motive, he told us you were already on the way to being well and truly smitten. I haven't heard my husband laugh so heartily since my Uncle Quentin forwarded us a jeweled camel saddle he had acquired somewhere in his many travels, just in case Patrick should ever decide to keep his own dromedary. I cannot tell you how let down I am to know that you aren't head over ears in love with the girl. And Patrick? Why, it is your dearest friend who might become suicidal at this news! For shame, Pierre. The least you could do is tell me you've been turned down by the creature and are even now in the midst of a sad decline.''

Pierre shook his head slowly. "Hanging is definitely too good for me,'' he drawled in his most deliberately maddening way. "Perhaps if I gave myself up to be boiled in oil it might, in some small way, earn me a measure of forgiveness in your eyes. Please, dearest Victoria, tell me how I can make you happy. I should not sleep nights, else.''

Victoria threw back her head and laughed. "Oh, Pierre, it really is good to be in your company again. Only you can deliver an insult in the form of an apology.''

He tipped his glass to her, smiling slightly. "Just as it is good to have you here, my good friend, someone who appreciates my feeble attempts at wit without being so thin-skinned as to be insulted.''

"Oh, dear.'' Victoria grimaced comically, then sobered. "Please don't tell me this Miss Caroline Addams— as your father tells me you call her—has no sense of humor. That really would be too bad of her, wouldn't it? But it is possible you are wrong, isn't it? I mean, I was once considered to be totally humorless, but that was only because there was so little to laugh about in my life. I believe I have made great strides, thanks to Patrick. Perhaps your Miss Addams has only misplaced her humor along with her memory? It is merely a thought, something to consider."

Pierre lifted a hand to absently stroke the small scar on his cheekbone. "I shall take your thoughts and suppositions under advisement," he agreed amicably, setting down his glass before rising and holding out a hand to her. "Your chamber should be ready by now, Victoria, if you'd like to refresh yourself."

She took his hand and also rose, to stand directly in front of him. "End of discussion, Pierre?" she asked, blighting him with her smile. "Very well, but only for now, and only because the trip has worn me to a frazzle, and I find I would very much like a lie-down on my bed. I shall reconvene my inquisition over the dining table tonight, when your Miss Addams is present."

"Was there ever any doubt of it?" Pierre countered, lifting her hand to his lips. "I have known you without funds, without future, without hope—but I have never known you without questions. It is good to see that you have brought the best of you into your new life, as I believe I would miss that inquisitive, incisive mind."

Victoria impetuously stood on tiptoe to kiss him on the cheek, something she wouldn't have even considered doing a few months earlier. "And to think that I once didn't believe I could like you," she quipped cheekily just as a loud commotion in the foyer turned both their heads in the direction of the doorway.

"Master Pierre! Master Pierre!" Hartley shouted, racing into the room. "You must come quickly. There's been a terrible accident."

"Accident?" Pierre asked curtly while Victoria noticed that the skin over his high cheekbones was suddenly drawn tight, his hold on her hand painfully snug. "What sort of accident?"

"A riding accident, Master Pierre," Hartley responded,

122

gasping for air, for he was not a young man anymore and was clearly overset with his news. "With Miss Addams's horse! She's been badly hurt. The groom just rode in to tell us that she's lying in the fields and—"

Pierre was already out of the room and bounding across the lawns to the stables, not hearing anything more, and Hartley was left to finish telling his story to Lady Wickford, who quickly led the old man to a chair and poured him a bracing cup of tea.

"Sir John Oakvale is with her, but the groom says she won't wake up, and she's terribly pale," Hartley told her, his hands shaking so badly that tea slopped onto the saucer. "I shouldn't be here, my lady, sitting with you. Oh, but it's wonderful of you to understand. My knees are shaking like dry bones in a sack. Why, if anything should happen to Miss Addams, Master Pierre might have all our heads!"

"He loves the young lady that much, then?" Victoria asked carefully, handing the butler a pristine white linen cloth with which to blot at the hot tea that had splashed onto his trousers.

Hartley bobbed his head emphatically. "He loves her dearly, my lady, and so all of us belowstairs say, except that Frenchie valet of Master Pierre's, Duvall, who doesn't love anything save his position."

"How very interesting," Victoria mused, turning to look out the window, as if she could see all the way to the field where Caroline lay unconscious, Pierre already racing to her side. "Then for everyone's sake, Hartley, I do hope she'll be all right."

She was floating in a truly wonderful dream, mercifully cut off from the world and its less than rosy realities, being carried high above the earth in the most gentle, comforting, safe embrace imaginable. There was no fear, no pain, no reason for worry or doubt. There was just peace, and the heady feeling of being totally and completely cherished. Even loved.

She hadn't always felt this peaceful, she knew. First

there had been the sickening sensation of falling, of losing her grip, followed by the painful buffeting of her body as her head and shoulders bounced about while her left leg was being pulled from its socket. Then terror had overwhelmed her, only to be superseded by the sure, unspoken, mind-destroying realization that she was about to die without ever having lived.

All this and more she had known in the space of a half-dozen heartbeats, then just as quickly forgotten at the moment she was lifted high against the chest of the strong angel who now held her to him, keeping her from harm, banishing all her fear, all her pain.

She moved her head slightly, wishing to press it against his chest, just to see if angels had heartbeats, too, and the pain came back, washing over her in wave after nauseating wave. She groaned aloud, unable to open her eyes but nevertheless sure she was no longer with the angel, but on a bed of nails instead, with a rock for her pillow.

"Caroline?" The voice she heard was low, masculine, and concerned. "Caroline, you're coming awake now, much as you would rather not, I'm sure. Open your eyes, Caroline. Please."

It was Pierre's voice she heard, although she was fully prepared to ignore it in the hope she might then be able to return to her lovely dream—that loving embrace. It was his last word that changed her mind, for that single, simple entreaty spoke volumes. He was worried about her. Poor man, she had caused him no end of trouble, hadn't she? She didn't want him to worry about her. She didn't want Pierre's concern, she wanted his—

"Pierre?" The voice was a whisper, a female whisper. "How is she? Before he left, Doctor Burgess was kind enough to tell me she should be fine, but that was hours ago. Shouldn't she be awake by now?"

It wasn't Mrs. Merrydell's voice. Caroline was sure of that. Mrs. Merrydell had an irritating, penetrating voice, like a pieman calling out his wares beneath her window. This voice was too sweet, too cultured to be that of her unfortunate choice of chaperone. Besides, the voice had called him Pierre, not Mr. Standish. No servant would do so, not even the encroaching Mrs. Merrydell.

Pierre must have turned slightly away from the bed to face the woman, for Caroline felt a slight tug on her hand, letting her know that he had been standing beside her, his hand wrapped snugly in hers. The realization that he had allowed this slight, unconscious intimacy had the effect of bringing stinging tears to her eyes.

"She stirred slightly just a moment ago, Victoria. Waking up will be painful for her, what with the blow to her head and the bruises on her back, which Burgess told me about, so I imagine she's fighting to stay unconscious."

Victoria. Who was Victoria? Caroline focused all her attention on the voices floating above her.

"You poor darling, you've been standing here all evening long, letting her hold your hand," Victoria said gently. "Please, at least let me get you a chair before you fall down. And you haven't eaten a thing."

Darling. She called him darling. Caroline didn't think she liked that.

"Thank you, but no. I'm fine. I can't ignore the fact that Caroline's had two bad blows to the head in such a short time. Stronger persons than she have been rendered permanently damaged. Why don't you retire now, my dear, you too have had quite a long day."

My dear. He called her my dear. Caroline liked that even less.

"I'm awake," she said abruptly, and not very civilly, knowing she just had to open her eyes and get a good look at "my dear" Victoria or else go mad. "I hope I'm not interrupting anything, but it's rather difficult to sleep when people insist on holding conversations within inches of my ear. Who are you?" she ended shortly, glaring up at Victoria.

Pierre stepped to one side, not letting loose his grip on Caroline's hand, and introduced Victoria to her.

"You're a countess?" Caroline heard herself asking stupidly. "I didn't know a countess could wear spectacles. At least not one so young and beautiful as you."

Victoria laughed and bent to kiss Caroline's cheek. "André told me you were outspoken, but I think I like you better this way than if you had been a simpering miss. I know I definitely like you better awake. You've had us all very worried, especially Pierre, who has stood by your side ever since carrying you home on his horse. How do you feel, Caroline? And, please, call me Victoria. My title is quite new and still makes me nervous."

Caroline's gaze shifted quickly to Pierre's face, not without pain. "You—you carried me?" she asked him, remembering again how safe she had felt, and marveling that she could ever have believed herself safe in his embrace. Safe was not a word she associated with this disturbing man. "Please allow me to thank you, Pierre," she said with dull politeness.

"So grudging, Caroline? One can only suppose you would rather I had left it to that brainless twit, Oatcake? He wanted to bring you home on a gate, doubtless finishing the job the fall began."

"His name is Oakvale, as you very well know," Caroline shot back, wondering if he actually believed it would injure him in some way to accept her thanks and be done with it. "Poor Sir John. He must have been very frightened by it all. I know I was. Not everyone can be as coolly detached as you, you know."

"I'll just leave you two to sort this out," Victoria interrupted, her voice tinged with humor as Pierre and Caroline glared at each other. "I'll stop by to see you in the morning, my dear. We really do have *so* much to talk about."

Caroline quickly murmured her good night to Victoria, still not knowing exactly who she was but content to wait till morning for an explanation. Right now all she could think of was her accident, an event that was more important to her at this moment than either Sir John's lack of good sense or Pierre's uncharacteristically gentle treatment of her injured body.

But any questions she might have had about her fall were to be delayed, for, as Victoria opened the door to the

126

hallway, Mrs. Merrydell charged into the room with, Caroline thought randomly, much the same grace that might be employed by a trumpeting rogue elephant trampling down some unfortunate native village that stood in its path.

"And it's about time, too!" Mrs. Merrydell exploded, her long strides eating up the space between door and bed in less than a heartbeat. "Whoever heard of the chaperone being forced to cool her heels in a hallway while the randy son of the household sits alone in a darkened bedchamber with a poor, defenseless girl? I'm half surprised her skirts aren't over her head, and that's a fact!"

Pierre stopped the woman in her tracks by the numbing frost of his black, icy stare. "Don't be vulgar, Mrs. Merrydell, or I shall be forced to have you removed—from the premises as well as from this room."

Mrs. Merrydell blustered for a moment or two, muttering random snatches such as "Well, I never—" and, "If you think for one moment that—" before ending quite humbly, "Please forgive me, sir. I'm quite overwrought with fear for poor, dear Miss Caroline."

"Of course you are," Pierre answered smoothly. "It is just, you see, that we would rather you were overwrought from a distance. You do understand me—don't you, dear Mrs. Merrydell?"

The woman looked about herself distractedly. "But—but—who will stay with her tonight? Surely, sir, you don't mean to—"

"Her maid will keep vigil," Pierre responded, earning himself a thankful squeeze of Caroline's hand on his. "Your duties do not include nursing, madam. And now, if you don't mind, Miss Caroline and I have something to discuss—in private."

Clearly Mrs. Merrydell was torn. One part of her wished for nothing more than to escape Pierre's piercing gaze with as much haste as possible, while another part of her dearly wished to remain, whether to protect her charge or to eavesdrop on some clandestine goings-on, Caroline couldn't be sure. In the end, personal protection won out, and Mrs. Merrydell retired, closing the door behind her so softly that it stayed open a crack.

Pierre saw the woman's lapse as well. He raised Caroline's hand to his lips, kissed it, and then released it to cross the room and firmly shut the door, turning the key in the lock. "The woman is necessary for the moment, but extremely tiresome," he remarked as he returned to Caroline's bedside and once more took up her hand, an unconscious gesture that immediately set her heart to pounding in her chest. "Are you up to talking about your accident just yet, Caroline, or shall I call your maid?"

"No, I want to talk," Caroline assured him hurriedly, struggling to sit up in bed. "Oh, my back!" she exclaimed as the slight exertion set off a small explosion of pain. "Did Lady step on me?"

"Doctor Burgess doesn't think so," Pierre told her, helping her to sit up by adjusting the pillows behind her head. "You were bruised by the rocks and stones you were dragged over until you were able to free your foot from the stirrup. According to Oakvale, you were a regular acrobat. I believe he has tumbled into love with you as a result, and would think it the best of good fun if you could run away together to join a traveling fair. He would, on consideration, make a tolerable juggler, wouldn't he?"

Caroline giggled, then caught herself up short as her chest ached. "That's not very nice, Pierre. Sir John thinks very highly of you."

Pierre let go of her hand to pull a chair over to the bed, but he did not sit down. "Don't defend him until you hear his latest bit of genius. It is Romeo Oatcake's considered opinion that, as one bump on the head served to remove your memory, this second bump has just as surely caused it to return. He was truly astonished that I had not thought of such a thing myself and conked you on your noggin a fortnight ago. When last I saw him he was preparing to call on you formally, only if your recovered memory means you have discovered that you are an heiress, of course. Not quite the sharpest knife in the cabinet, is he, poor fellow?"

128

"Of course," Caroline answered distractedly, ignoring his disparaging remarks about Sir John's brainpower, her mind busy with other thoughts. "Although I certainly wasn't actively seeking another bump on my head, and appreciate the fact that you abstained from giving me one, Sir John's idea does hold some merit. What one bump took away, another bump just might return. Except for one thing. I haven't remembered anything more. As far as I know, my name is Caroline Addams and my life began the day you found me in the roadway."

She looked over at Pierre, her clear blue-violet eyes narrowed thoughtfully. "But *you* couldn't have known that until I told you. That would be impossible. Wouldn't it?"

Chapter Fourteen

"I don't know, Caroline. Would it be possible? Perhaps I am fey. My maternal grandmother was originally from a small village in County Cork, and you know what has been said about the Irish."

"Don't try to fob me off with any of your nonsense, Pierre," Caroline warned, pouting. "There is just no way you could know whether I had regained my memory or not without me telling you. Unless,"—she stopped for a moment, her features assembling themselves in a thoughtful frown—"unless you know something you're not telling me." She sniffed derisively. "Of course you do! It would be just like you, wouldn't it? Oh yes, that's you all right, straight down to the ground. Sneaky and underhanded."

"How you do go on," Pierre drawled, resting his palm on her forehead and peering down at her assessingly. "Perhaps you have picked up a touch of fever. It isn't uncommon, I'm told, in people with delicate constitutions—and those who persist in trying to attack rocks with their heads. Why don't you get a good night's rest, and we can talk again in the morning."

"I don't want to talk in the morning—I want to talk *now!*" Caroline removed his hand from her brow with some force, ignoring the renewed slab of pain the impulsive movement caused her. "How did you know I hadn't regained my memory?"

Pierre thought quickly, searching his agile brain for some reasonably believable explanation that would fob her off—at least until he could come up with a more convincing fib. Then he sighed, letting her know he was giving in to her much the way a weary parent does when it can stand a child's whining no longer. "Very well, brat," he relented, "but you won't like it. You see, it was your eyes."

"My eyes? What have my eyes got to do with anything? You know, this is just like you, Pierre. You're not making any sense."

"On the contrary, I am making sense, or at least I do when I am allowed to speak more than two words without being interrupted by a mannerless infant."

"I'm so prodigiously sorry," Caroline spat, not sorry in the least. "Please go on with your explanation, I shan't interrupt."

"Yes, you will," Pierre contradicted, lightly flicking his index finger across the tip of her nose. "You live to interrupt me. I imagine, in fact, that it has become one of your premier pleasures in life. But as I said, it was your eyes that told me. When you opened them they were still quite blank."

"Blank! How dare you! As if it weren't enough to relegate me to the role of puling infant, now you must make me sound like some brainless ninny!"

Pierre tilted his head in her direction and pointed a finger at her, wordlessly reminding her that he had said she would interrupt him. "You are never stupid, Caroline," he corrected her. "But if the blow to your head had served to shake your memory loose, you would have awakened with your eyes filled with wonder, not blank with incomprehension. It's simple, really, with no mystery involved, no hidden secrets."

"And if I believe you, will you promise to let me jump Obtuse over a five-bar gate once I'm recovered?" she countered, letting him know she had not swallowed his obvious bag of moonshine. "However, I will allow myself to be satisfied with your explanation—for now. What really concerns me is the way the girth came loose the moment I put Lady into a gallop. I can't bring myself to believe that the groom was careless. He is too good at what he does."

Pierre surprised her with a small bow. "I make you my compliments, imp, and shall convey your high praise to the groom, who has been desolated by your tumble. Even with your brains addled from your latest injury you have been able to deduce the fact that your accident was—dare I say it?—no accident."

All thoughts of her headache and painful back faded instantly as Caroline's attention narrowed to exclude everything except the digestion of this latest piece of information. "No accident? But how—why?"

Pierre sat on the side of the bed, taking the hand she had impulsively held out to him. "The how of it is very simple. Both sides of the leather strap had been shaved, not so much as to be noticed by the groom, but just enough so that the cinch was not a true fit and would begin to slide open once you put Lady into a gallop. It was not a matter of *if* you would fall, but *when*. The method was woefully unoriginal, not the sort of thing to inspire my awe, but it was effective just the same."

"Whoever committed the deed would doubtless be forever cast down to learn that the great Pierre Standish was not overly impressed with his technique," Caroline pronounced in accents of disgust. "You would have been much more prone to voice your appreciation of his efforts had I been killed, I'm sure."

Pierre squeezed her hand, smiling. "Poor little Caroline. Forgive me, brat. A disdain for mediocrity, even in villains, is my besetting sin. In truth, I should have been inconsolable had you died."

"You say that with the same feeling you'd give to voicing your displeasure over the second remove at dinner," Caroline complained pettishly, tugging hard to free her hand from his grasp, but he wouldn't let her go.

"Think, my dear hothead. Don't let your anger with me distract you from the point," he warned quietly.

Her hand stilled in his, and she looked at him closely, her huge eyes opened wide. "Someone's trying to kill me, aren't they, Pierre?"

He nodded, his gaze not leaving hers. "Either one

someone, or perhaps even two someones. It's not exactly a revelation though, is it, considering the first attempt in the gardens?''

"Then you really *do* believe someone wants me dead?'' Although Caroline had considered just such an idea many times since the incident in the gardens, hearing it spoken out loud, and by Pierre Standish, who didn't seem to ever believe in *anything*, frightened her more than she thought possible. "But who—and why?''

Pierre took a deep breath, and let it out in a weary sigh. "We progress, I see, from how and why to who and why. Unfortunately, I have precious few answers for you. All I can say for now is that you obviously are a great deal of bother to someone—besides me, that is—and that someone would very much like to have you removed from the face of the earth. It's a terrible thing, isn't it, to have enemies?''

"You ought to know,'' Caroline groused, as his words had only served to sink her spirits lower than before. "You must have acquired dozens of them over the years with your winning ways. But that's nothing to the point, is it? What do we do now?''

"*We* don't do anything,'' he told her, ignoring her sarcasm. "You are to lie here until you feel completely recovered, and then you are to go about your business just as you have been doing, taking care not to outrun your groom or wander away from the house without Victoria in tow. That is why Father sent her here, you know, crafty devil that he is. I do not consider the so volatile Mrs. Merrydell sufficient protection no matter how ferocious her demeanor, so please do not consider yourself safe if you are alone with her. Leave it to Father and me to ferret out the bogeyman responsible for your 'accidents.' ''

Caroline was livid. "Do you really believe I can know what I know now and just stand back and put my safety into your hands, without lifting a finger to save myself? Well, I refuse to be treated as if I were incapable of defending myself. You must be out of your mind, Pierre Standish! How can you possibly expect me to—*oh!*''

Pierre's mouth swooped down on hers, effectively shutting off her tirade before, his lips still on hers, he lowered her gently onto the pillows by her shoulders, being careful not to touch her tender back before raising his hands to cup either side of her face. His thumbs worked gently against her soft cheeks, molding her to him and wordlessly urging her mouth to open beneath his so that he could deepen the kiss.

Against her will, if indeed she'd had any will left to summon, Caroline felt her arms sliding up around Pierre's neck and gloried in the warm solidness of him as his firm body pressed lightly against her tingling breasts. His tongue was foreign to her, but a welcome stranger, introducing itself by way of quick, teasing thrusts, its slightly raspy texture stroking the roof of her mouth. She reached out to meet it, the touch of warm, wet flesh against warm, wet flesh causing an extraordinary explosion deep inside her.

Pierre felt her daring exploration and shuddered convulsively, longing to crush her completely against him in order to convince himself that she was truly all right.

Only that afternoon he had thought he'd lost her, had thought that his arrogant manipulations had failed to protect her. The possibility of losing Caroline had nearly driven him mad as he had ridden out on Obtuse, not caring for the animal's safety as he urged the stallion to fly over the ground to where Caroline lay.

If there had been any questions, any lingering doubts in his mind as to exactly how he felt toward his Good Deed, they had all been laid to rest during the terrible ride.

He loved her. He didn't know how, he didn't know when; he only knew that she had come into his life unwanted, unlooked for, and had become the most important, the most valuable part of it. And he'd die before he let anyone hurt her.

Even himself.

This last thought brought Pierre back to a realization of what he was doing. He pulled away from her slowly, regretfully, looking deeply into her tear-washed eyes before

134

closing his own for a sanity-restoring moment, shaking his head. He had said too much, frightening her, and now his ill-timed passion had frightened her even more.

"Pierre?" Caroline's voice was very small, very confused.

He smiled, deliberately lifting his left eyebrow in the mocking way she had told him infuriated her. "Sorry, darling. I am a brute, but it's the only way I've ever known to silence a beautiful female when she's talking too much. I'll leave you now so that you can get some well-earned rest. Victoria will be tippy-toeing in here as early as is decent tomorrow morning, to plague you with a million or more questions of her own."

Caroline's tears spilled over to run down her pale cheeks, but he ignored them, turning for the door.

"But—but—" she began, reaching out to him. Suddenly, reason rushed back into her brain and she flushed with shame. "I detest you, Pierre Standish," she called after his departing back, knowing no other response except anger. "Do you hear me? I *detest* you!"

He didn't answer.

Once Susan had satisfied herself that her charge was settled comfortably for the night, and only moments before Caroline was pushed to the point of screaming by the maid's affectionate fussing, she was left to turn her head into her pillow and quietly cry herself to sleep while, downstairs, in the privacy of his father's study, Pierre drank his brandy slowly, far into the dark hours of the night.

The sound of the slap, the sharp sting of flesh connecting with flesh, echoed through the small clearing, scattering a pair of birds who had been resting in the branches of a nearby tree.

"*Ouch!*" Ursley Merrydell exclaimed in a high, whining voice, his hand flying to his cheek to rub the tingling skin. "I knew you were going to do that, from the minute I found out that the stupid girl didn't die. You always do that. Why do you always do that?"

135

His mother, who was feeling only slightly mollified by her physical display of temper, shot back angrily, *"Why* do I always do that, Ursley? It's a wonder you should ask. I always do that because you always fail—*that's* why. I beg one simple favor of you, one simple little murder, but do you do it? No, you don't. 'As simple as falling off a horse,' that's what you said. Only it wasn't so simple, was it?" She slapped him again, on the shoulder, just for good measure. "I had such high hopes for you, Ursley, I really did. But you're just like your father. He could never get the straight of anything either."

Panic invaded Ursley's stringy body, turning his bony knees to water. He didn't want to be compared to his father. His father had failed once too often—and his father had been eliminated. "No, Mother, don't say that!" he protested on a sob, dropping to his knees at her feet. "Didn't I do just as you said at the cobbler's?"

Amity softened, for Ursley was her son, and she loved him. Really she did—at least most of the time. It was just at times like these, when she was on the hunt, that she tended to conveniently misplace her motherly instincts.

She bent down to pat his cheek affectionately, ignoring his involuntary wince. "Of course you did, my darling boy. You were just wonderful at the cobbler's. I was very proud of you. It's just that I had so hoped she would die when the saddle slipped. It was just an unfortunate accident; you couldn't have known she'd be able to throw herself clear of the horse's hooves, now could you?"

"No, Mama," Ursley agreed hurriedly, clambering to his feet, knowing from experience that the worst was over and they would be able to talk now. "I couldn't know that. But—but what do we do now? I won't be able to get near the stables again. Standish is sure to post guards."

But Amity wasn't listening. She was still suffering from one of her increasingly rare bouts of motherly affection. She inspected her son for signs of illness, turning his face this way and that as she held his cheeks painfully tight between thumb and forefinger. "Are you sleeping well, my dear boy? You look a mite pulled. You aren't letting that cheeky serving wench have her wicked way with you, are you, while Mama's not close by to watch out for you? You could catch something, you know, and a whopping dose of the pox wouldn't do either one of us a dram's worth of good.''

Ursley hid his eyes, knowing they would reveal the fact that the ungrateful wench at the inn was still turning down his every offer. She'd even poured an entire pitcher of ale over his head the last time he had tried to win her favor with a well-placed pinch. "I wouldn't have anything to do with the slut, Mama. I'm a good boy. You know that. Besides, we're here on business.''

They *were* in the middle of a piece of business, and Ursley's reminder brought Amity's mind back to the matter at hand. She released his face, leaving Ursley to gratefully massage his cheeks, and began to pace as she thought out loud. "Standish is getting suspicious. He'd have to be dumb as a red brick not to be, I suppose, but I don't much like the way he's been looking at me. And he makes sure I'm never alone with her. I'm beginning to have a bad feeling about this. We have to move fast or lose everything.''

Ursley nodded, happy to step in and take charge now that his mother had admitted she had been feeling some qualms of her own. "You'll have to do it yourself," he said, beginning to pace in step with her. "Slip something nasty into her tea, or something. We can't count on her not remembering you sooner or later and setting up a hollering that will bring Pierre Standish on the double. Then there'll be the very devil to pay, and I won't be able to help you.''

Amity turned on her son, cold fury in her eyes. "No, you wouldn't, would you? You'd be on a coach heading away from here just as fast as you could. You'd go to America, wouldn't you? Oh yes, I've seen your face when you talk about those golden streets over there. Well, let me tell you a thing or two, my fine young man. If I go to prison I won't go alone. You'll be right there beside me!''

Ursley frowned, for this was a sobering thought indeed.

He was convinced he would not like prison above half, and a ride to prison shared with his free-swinging mother could prove to be an extremely painful journey. "Nothing will go wrong," he assured her as he tried to reassure himself. "The third time's the charm, as they say. You'll find the perfect thing to do and we'll be on our way to wealth and a life of ease. Just you wait, Mama. We'll have the best of everything, exactly like you always promised. It'll be grand!"

Amity Merrydell smiled and allowed herself to be mollified. Her son was right. She was forgetting that he was his father's son, a born bungler. It was her turn now. The girl was as good as below ground.

Chapter Fifteen

"*En voilà une affaire!*"

"Jaw bangin' ter yerself in that froggie croak agin, are yer?" Jeremy commented, looking up from the boot he had been polishing with more energy than effect as the valet stormed into the workroom, slamming the door shut behind him in a show of temper. "Yer always gripin' 'bout somethin', like some ol' biddy leanin' over a washtub. Now wot's stickin' in yer craw?"

"I have not the cat in my throat," Duvall denied angrily, abruptly grabbing his master's favorite riding boot from the young boy's hands and taking up a clean polishing rag, intent on demonstrating the correct way to put a mirror finish on the costly leather. "And do not dare to speak to me so of my language, *mouffette*. Your language, it is of *la poubelle,* the garbage."

Jeremy eyed the valet narrowly, knowing he wanted to learn how to be a gentlman's gentleman, yet hating the fact that his beloved guv'nor had seen fit to place him under Duvall's tutelage. His short sojourn as a fledgling groom having come to a bad end—a circumstance having much to do with a certain, truly unlikable groom (who had endeavored to administer his instructions to the former chimney sweep with the toe of his boot) having discovered a prodigious amount of ripe manure in his cot—Jeremy knew his master's hopes were aimed a smidgeon too high, but he longed to make the man proud of him anyway.

Jeremy's loyalty to Pierre, always strong, had increased tenfold with the rousting of Hawkins the sweep, and the thought of failing his guv'nor again distressed him mightily; so much so that he now said, "Oi'm sorry, Frenchie, truly Oi am. Oi'll do better, 'onest Oi will."

"It is not of your miserable self that I speak," Duvall informed him, shoving the shined boot under Jeremy's nose and turning it this way and that, so that the leather would gleam in the sunlight. "It is this affair of the name-less lady, this Miss Addams. She will be the death of my master. I feel it here,"—he beat the polishing rag against his breast for emphasis—"in my heart."

Jeremy, who had heard of Caroline's fall from a horse the day before, seemed to be of the opinion that, if the lady persisted in tumbling onto her head it would be *she* who would be carried to bed on six men's shoulders, not his beloved guv'nor. He said as much to Duvall, who im-mediately cuffed him across the top of his short, golden fuzz.

"Ow! Yer villain!" the lad exclaimed, rubbing his head. "Wot yer do that fer? Yer always after m' 'ead, ain't yer, some ways or otter?"

"I only hope for to knock some sense into it," Duvall answered reasonably, pulling a short stool beside the boy and squatting down on it so that he could see Jeremy as well as talk to him. "I don't mean the master will die, you fool. And it won't be the girl who will perish, so much the pity. Didn't you listen with your fat cabbage ears when the master told us to watch with both eyes the Merrydell woman who is trying to harm her? No, it is not an end of life of which I speak. It is my master's heart I worry for."

Jeremy's head snapped up, and he looked straight at the valet, grinning wickedly. "Billin' an' cooin' are they? Yer'd better watch yer steps, Frenchie, or she'll toss yer out on yer ear when she snags 'im. Guv'nor won't take kindly ter yer iffen yer bad-mouth 'is missus. Me, Oi like 'er fine, an' guv'nor knows it. *Oi'm* safe, Oi am. Yer won't find Jeremy 'Olloway back in Piccadilly!"

Duvall's sallow skin flushed an unhealthy orange. "I never said I did not like Miss Addams," he corrected rapidly. "It's just that we get along so well, the master and me, and I do not look forward to a petticoat household."

Jeremy nodded his understanding. "Nothin' worse than wimmen. Always wantin' ter be boss, an' all. But Miss Addams is straight up. Yer won't get no trouble from 'er, iffen yer can learn ter keep yer yapper shut."

Duvall hopped to his feet, not knowing if he was angry with Jeremy, who couldn't see the handwriting on the wall, or with himself, for being dull-witted enough to think the simpleton would understand his problems. He and Pierre made a good team, and had done so for years. A woman would ruin everything; probably even want a gaggle of children about, drooling on his master's spotless waistcoat. *"Va te faire cuire un oeuf!"* he spat in Gallic fury, turning away before he did Jeremy an injury.

"Huh?" the boy questioned blankly as he righted the stool Duvall had kicked over in his fury.

Duvall turned back to level Jeremy with a look that brooked no argument. "You know nothing, less than nothing! I said for you to go cook yourself an egg!" Then he stormed out of the workroom to nurse his present and anticipated wounds in the privacy of his small sanctum located behind Pierre's dressing room.

Jeremy scratched the side of his head. Cook himself an egg? He sighed, feeling slightly sad in spite of himself. It was obvious the valet was slipping round the bend. If he, Jeremy Holloway, wished to remain under the man's tutelage, and in the house—where there was not a bit of horse manure to be found, let alone shoveled into piles—he had better be extra nice to him, for the man's mind was about to snap. He set down the half-polished boot and headed for the kitchens, intent on boiling a fresh egg.

Lady Wickford knocked softly on the door, then lifted the latch and poked her head inside the room, peeking toward the bed that stood in the shadows at the far side of the chamber. "Caroline?" she questioned in a loud whisper. "Are you awake?"

Caroline, who had been awake for hours, remained very

141

still, hoping her visitor would take the hint and go away. She was not up to facing the countess. She was not up to facing anyone. She just wanted to lie there, in the darkness, until everyone forgot about her.

Her eyes tightly closed, she sensed rather than saw Victoria beside her bed. "Caroline? It's past noon. Surely you should be hungry?"

Sighing, Caroline turned her head in Victoria's direction, still refusing to open her eyes. "I am never going to eat again," she vowed quietly but firmly.

Victoria laughed, pulling up a small chair so that she could make herself comfortable. "Pierre does have that effect at times, doesn't he?" she remarked kindly. "It is Pierre you are hiding from, isn't it? He's a difficult man to understand, I know, but he cares very deeply for you, although I'm sure you don't believe me."

Caroline opened her eyes and looked up at Victoria. "You're right. I don't believe you."

Victoria settled back in her chair, arranging her skirts over her knees. "Then I imagine you wouldn't be interested in hearing how Pierre behaved when he was told that you had suffered an accident. Pity," she said, sighing. "It was quite a remarkable reaction from a man who has made it a rule never to react to anything. Ah, you're sitting up. Wonderful. Perhaps you will decide to have a small meal?"

Caroline ignored this second offer of food, her entire attention directed to Victoria's hint that Pierre had been worried about her. "What did he do?" she asked curiously, leaning toward her visitor. "Was he truly upset? I remember you saying something about it being Pierre who carried me here—and he held my hand, didn't he? I didn't dream it all, I'm convinced of that."

Victoria used the tip of her index finger to push her spectacles more firmly onto the bridge of her nose. She was enjoying herself, and only wished her dearest Patrick could be here as well, to share in the fun. "Pierre was distraught from the moment he heard the terrible news until you finally awoke, Caroline. He was totally unhinged. He bellowed at the doctor—at all of us—and threatened anyone who came close to you with bodily harm, caring for you himself.'' She lifted her chin, smiling at the memory. "It was wonderful to see. I always wondered if Pierre were human, and now I know that he is. I should have known it would take a woman to bring a man such as he fully to life.''

Caroline reached out a hand, found Victoria's, and squeezed it hard. "Thank you, my friend,'' she said, blinking away tears. "I needed to hear that. He confuses me so, you understand,'' she admitted, "kissing me one moment and treating me as if I were an annoying rash the next. I never know where I stand with him, or what he wants of me.''

"Kissing you?'' Victoria repeated interestedly. "He hasn't—''

Caroline shook her head vehemently. "No, *no!* Of course not! Pierre would *never*—that is, I wouldn't *allow*—not that he *tried* to—''

Victoria waved her hands, signaling her understanding. "I didn't think so, my dear, but as a married woman, and supposedly conventional, I had to ask. I remember Patrick—'' She hesitated, intent on a memory of her own courtship. "But Pierre is an honorable man,'' she ended firmly. "If he has kissed you, you and he are as good as affianced.''

Now Caroline's tears came in earnest, for there was nothing she would love more than to be married to Pierre. She loved him, infuriating, secretive despot that he was, and she could almost believe he loved her, too, in his own way. But whom did he love? She was a nameless nobody, and as if that in itself were not enough, somebody was trying to kill her. What sort of future could the two of them have with such a terrible cloud hanging over their heads?

It was impossible, and so she told Victoria, who listened politely and then replied in her most officious tone: "Poppycock! Pierre would never let anyone hurt you, so that is one problem as good as solved, although I will admit you had a close call yesterday. I believe Pierre spent most of last night kicking himself for that, so he will be twice as protective from this point on, until the person or persons who wish you harm are unearthed and punished.''

''And my memory?'' Caroline questioned, Victoria's matter-of-fact solutions amazing her. ''Can you solve that problem so easily as well?''

''Your memory will return any day now, as I have read extensively on just this sort of phenomenon, and your chances of a full recovery are extremely high. I am not one who puts much credence in prophecy, but I do believe I am in this case allowed to say with full conviction that you and Pierre will then marry and remove to London, where you will become the darling of Society and Pierre will astonish all who know him by doting on you night and day.''

Caroline shook her head. ''You make it all sound so simple. You've really read about cases like mine?'' she asked, this part of Victoria's conversation completely penetrating her brain. She looked closely at the woman, noting once more the wire-rimmed spectacles and the sharp intelligence lurking behind them. ''Are you a bluestocking, Victoria?''

''I was,'' she told her, winking. ''I've retired from all that now, content to be a wife and, if my sudden aversion to my morning chocolate is any indication of my condition, soon to be a mother. If you don't mind my saying so, I believe you might be just a tad blue yourself, Caroline. You're certainly no featherheaded miss, even if Pierre tells me your education must have come at the hands of a person who didn't mind his speech in front of you.''

After congratulating Victoria most sincerely, and thanking her for traveling by coach to come to Pierre's aid while in her delicate condition, Caroline broached a subject she had been longing to discuss with someone. ''Last night, when everyone was talking above my head, I thought that they were as loud as the pieman calling outside my window. Piemen don't hawk their wares in the country, do they? It must mean that I have lived in London.''

Nodding, Victoria added, ''Or some other town of rea-

144

sonable size. I told you that you were quick. Another young woman wouldn't have realized that the pieman was a valuable clue. Let me ring for a tray before you tell me what else you have discovered."

Pierre sat behind his father's desk, the fingertips of his right hand rhythmically drumming on the tabletop. It had been too close, this last attack. He had been cutting it too fine, trying to play his cards closely to his vest and not allowing anyone else in on his plans. His secrecy had cost him, and Caroline. He couldn't make another mistake.

He stopped his drumming to open the top drawer of the desk and remove the letter he had received from his father more than a week earlier. Unfolding the single sheet, he read over the missive, nodding his silent agreement with his father's conclusions, then shaking his head as he reread the last line.

"No, Father, I'm afraid I cannot do that any longer," he said aloud. "I cannot wait for your return before putting an end to this nonsense. It has proved too dangerous." He refolded the paper and replaced it in the drawer, then rose to stare out the window overlooking the gardens.

How long he stood there he didn't know, but when he turned around once more it was to see his father standing before him, still dressed in his traveling cape and hat.

"Good afternoon, my son," André said by way of greeting, still in the process of stripping off his gloves. "You look like the very devil, if I might say so without fear of being tossed out of my own home on my ear."

"Good afternoon, Father," Pierre returned calmly, automatically concealing any shock André's sudden reappearance might have caused. He hadn't heard a carriage draw up, or been aware of any commotion in the foyer. "You've had a pleasant journey, I trust."

"Yes, indeed," André agreed. "I had quite forgotten the myriad joys of traveling about the countryside by coach, making do with post horses, sleeping between damp linen, and picking at indifferent meals. You may kiss me if you wish, although I'd rather you didn't, as displays of

145

affection can be so wearing. How fares our Miss Addams?''

Pierre averted his eyes from his father's penetrating stare, preferring to cross to the drinks table and pour them each a small glass of wine. "She had a small accident with her horse yesterday," he told him as he handed over one of the glasses. "The saddle cinch had been shaved." Lifting his own drink to his lips, he drained the liquid in one swallow and then hurled the glass into the cold fireplace. "Playtime's over, Father."

"She will recover." André stated, didn't question, for he already knew the answer. If any permanent harm had come to Caroline, Pierre would have had his head by now and not just contented himself with destroying a fine piece of French crystal. "Forgive me, my son. It now seems I sadly underestimated our adversaries, and led you to do likewise. They appear to be more than mere bumbling nuisances. We have no more time to hope for Caroline to recover her memory on her own."

He stripped off his hat and cloak and flung them carelessly onto a nearby chair in preparation of getting down to business. "May I presume that the Merrydell is still walking among us, or have you got her hanging by her thumbs in the cellars?"

Pierre shot his father a piercing look. "She and the son met for a heated conference this morning among the trees at the bottom of the gardens, but she's back in the house now. I've given orders that she is to be watched at all times and is not allowed to see Caroline alone. I think she'll try poison next, if she listens to her son, whom she seems alternately to adore and detest. I only wish I could have overheard all of their conversation, as I cannot yet fathom how they plan to handle identifying Caroline's body and claiming the money. After all, Mrs. Merrydell certainly can't suddenly pretend she has recognized her ward, can she? I have to own it, Father, the woman is beginning to get on my nerves."

"Yes. I had noticed that." André retired to the chair behind his desk and sat down, steepling his fingers as he leaned his elbows on the desktop. "She's not suspicious?"

Pierre shook his head derisively. "Our dear Mrs. Merrydell is too sure of herself, too single-minded in her mission, to be suspicious, although we cannot rely on her overweening stupidity for much longer." He walked over to the desk and perched on one corner. "Must I beg, Father, or are you going to tell me who Caroline really is? Surely you know by now. You seem to know everything else."

"Tsk, tsk, Pierre," André could not refrain from teasing. "It isn't like you to be so precipitate. I do believe I like it. Your Good Deed has been all that I could have hoped. I think I'll just toddle upstairs to thank her personally. I wouldn't wish to be rude, you understand. And then there's dear Lady Wickford. I should be very shabby indeed if I didn't clean up my dirt and present her my compliments as soon as may be." He rose, placing his palms on the desktop. "You will excuse me, Pierre, won't you?"

"I'd have a lesser man's heart for a paperweight," Pierre returned cheerfully enough, "but I'll allow you to play out your string as long as it pleases you, Father, with only a word of caution. My patience grows thin."

André leaned across the desk to tap his son on the cheek. "Humility. That's the ticket, *mon fils*. You've come a long way. Now, what say we dispense with these melodramatic displays of affection so that I might retire to change before we visit the ladies. Victoria is with her, I imagine, standing guard?

Pierre bowed his head, silently counting to ten. He had earned this, he knew, all this and more, for having doubted his father, for having doubted his mother's constant love. But, oh, how it hurt to have to stand back and let the older man call all the moves. Yet, if it had been left to him he would have done much the same, right up until the moment he knew his heart to be committed.

Now, the moves, the strategies, the thrill of the hunt, seemed no more than childish games, and more than a little dangerous. At last he understood why Patrick Sherbourne had seen so little humor in Victoria's quest to find Quennel Quinton's murderer.

When love enters the picture, the thrill of the game flies directly out the window.

"Coming, Father," Pierre heard himself saying dutifully, just as Jeremy Holloway erupted into the room without bothering to knock.

"Guv'nor! Guv'nor! She put somethin' in the tea. Oi wuz boilin' an egg, jist like Frenchie said ter do—'es so tip-top, knowin' just wot Oi should do—an' Oi seen 'er plain wit m' daylights, that bracket-faced bubby, sneakin' sumthin' inter missy's teapot. Oi came right 'ere, jist like yer said ter do, ter tell yer. Yer coulda knocked me flat— that Frenchie is fly!'' Catching his breath, Jeremy turned to see André Standish in the room and quickly tugged at his nonexistent forelock. "Oh, 'ello there, Whitey. Oi didn't 'ear yer wuz back."

"My lapse entirely, young man," André confessed dryly. "Henceforth I shall make it clear you are to be informed of all my arrivals and departures. But for now, with your kind permission and with heartfelt thanks for your keen eyesight and steadfast loyalty, I find that I have matters to which I must attend."

Jeremy gave a negligent wave of his hand. "Be m' guest, Whitey. Oi gots ter get back ter m' egg anyways."

Pierre and his father exchanged gazes, then both walked rapidly toward the stairs.

Chapter Sixteen

They entered the chamber without knocking, two perfectly dressed gentlemen whose physical presence displayed the best of their generations, from the understated elegance of their well-cut clothing, to the athletic healthfulness of their bodies, to the light of intelligence that burned so brightly in their dark eyes.

Once more Caroline was struck by their close physical resemblance: André, who proved that a gentleman can age without losing one iota of his attractiveness, and Pierre, who was enjoying the full flower of his manhood. But more than their physical likenesses, Caroline was once again aware of the uncanny, silent communication they shared.

Pierre had taken no more than three steps into the room before he saw Victoria standing to one side of Caroline's bed, neatly pouring the contents of a full china teapot into the base of a large potted plant. As he turned to André, who had also seen Victoria, the two men visibly relaxed, their bodies unknowingly mimicking each other in the way they immediately became more slack of shoulder, less aggressive in their step; their dark eyes became instantly shuttered, their entire posture changing from controlled haste to smiling congeniality, radiating a mood of ease and even slight boredom.

"Good day, ladies," André said, stopping just short of the bed where Caroline rested, a half-dozen pillows propped at her back. He bowed from the waist. "Please excuse our precipitate entrance, my dears, but I was so overcome with eagerness to see both you dear people again that I completely misplaced my good manners. Victoria, you are positively glowing. May I presume that you are planning to present dearest Patrick with a token of your affection, as we so politely phrase it? Caroline, you naughty puss, I hear you have taken a tumble. Shall we have to relegate you to using my late wife's dogcart?''

Caroline, recovering from her momentary awe, mumbled a curt welcome, then narrowed her eyes and looked past André to where Pierre stood, idly inspecting one lace shirtcuff, and announced baldly, ''Mrs. Merrydell brought me tea and Victoria dumped it on a plant, which I do believe is already showing signs of wilting. I know that ladies in my new friend's delicate condition are at times prone to eccentricities, but I doubt this is one of them. Would you care to offer me an explanation, Pierre, or am I going to be forced to draw my own conclusions?''

''A flush hit, I'd say,'' André remarked, looking at his son.

''There's nothing wrong with her eyesight,'' Victoria slipped in, sitting down once more and replacing the empty teapot on the silver tray Mrs. Merrydell had delivered. ''And hello to you, dearest André. You look fine as ninepence, even in your traveling clothes.''

Pierre stepped forward. ''Ah, poor Father,'' he drawled, ignoring Caroline's demands. ''You have just been reprimanded; quite gently, but reprimanded none the less. We will be happy to excuse you, of course, if you wish to go to your rooms and change out of your dirt.''

''No, we won't,'' Caroline piped up, quickly sitting up, as if ready to bound from the bed and physically restrain the man.

''We won't?'' Pierre questioned, eyeing her warily. ''Are you going to prove tiresome, brat?''

''We won't,'' she repeated firmly, ignoring his insult. ''What you will do is gather round my bed like good little soldiers—as I am reluctant to leave it until my back feels less like Lady has stepped on it with all four feet—and tell me just what the devil is going on!''

''She seems a bit grumpy, my son,'' André commented

kindly. "One can always tell, because her language slips a notch. Rather endearing, don't you think? Yet, all things considered, perhaps another visit from the good doctor is in order?"

"Yes, she does seem sadly out of coil," Pierre agreed. "I suggest we retire, you to change and me to summon Doctor Burgess, while Victoria fetches a cold cloth with which to bathe Caroline's fevered brow."

"Don't bother the doctor, Pierre," Caroline broke in, her voice rather strained. "I believe my agitation is easily diagnosed. As a matter of fact, I am convinced it is due to something I *almost* drank."

Victoria stood. "Oh, give it up, gentlemen," she told them, laughing. "The time has come to make a clean breast of things. Caroline wants some answers. As she has borne the brunt of the thing, being subjected to attempts on her life, I do believe she is not making an out-of-the-way demand. Besides, knowing only half the story thus far, I too am curious. André, have you been able to discover her identity since last we met?"

Caroline couldn't be sure, but she thought André hesitated for a moment, less than half a heartbeat actually, before shaking his head. "I am mortified to admit that I have not—at least not definitely." He brightened slightly as he looked directly at her and added, "I'm close, I am convinced of it. I lack only one last verifying communication from my man in Leicester, where I am fairly certain you lived. I would have traveled there myself, except for my strong desire to be back with you here at Standish Court."

"Leicester?" Victoria questioned, turning to Caroline. "That would explain the pieman." She turned to the older Standish. "Your 'man,' André? He is on his way here now, I trust?"

"On winged feet, my dear," André assured her, winking.

"Leicester. That is miles north of London, I'm sure, and so far away from here," Caroline added, looking puzzled. "Surely I could not have traveled from there bare-

151

foot. It must be some mistake. I couldn't possibly have come from Leicester."

"You make it sound dreadful, imp. Leicester is a lovely place," Pierre broke in smoothly, "although its history is sometimes bloodthirsty. If I'm correct, Richard III passed the night before the Battle of Bosworth there, in the Blue Boar Inn, and his body was buried in the Grey Friars' church. Poor, abused man. Eventually his remains were exhumed and tossed into the Soar from Bow Bridge and his stone coffin turned into a horse trough, possibly for use at that same Blue Boar Inn. Still, all things considered," he ended as Caroline's steely stare threatened to skewer him where he stood, "it is, as I said, a delightful city."

"Founded by King Lear, I believe, on the site of the Roman *Ratae*," André, barely containing his mirth, added helpfully, earning himself a steely stare of his own.

Pierre nodded. "Ah, yes, there is a wealth of history in Leicester. But we digress. I believe I hear dearest Caroline gnashing her teeth."

"I think you are both abominable!" Caroline declared vehemently, reaching behind her to toss a pillow in their general direction. *"Ouch!* My back! Now see what you've made me do! There are times when I think I have lost my memory, and other times when I'm equally convinced I am only suffering from delusions, and that none of this is real. I'm not in Sussex, surrounded by village idiots—save Victoria, who has been the best of good friends to me. I'm actually in Bedlam, *imagining* all of this!"

Victoria retrieved the pillow and placed it behind Caroline, gently pushing her against it while asking her to please not exert herself any further. She, Victoria promised in an undertone, would handle matters from here.

When she turned to face the Standishes, she was no longer Victoria Sherbourne, Countess of Wickford, but Victoria Quinton, master sleuth. "All right, gentlemen," she began, pulling herself up to her full height and glaring commandingly at them from behind her spectacles, "let's get down to cases, shall we? Restricting ourselves to only what is known for a fact, and not straying to conjecture or

152

supposition—or even enlightening lessons in ancient history—just precisely what *do* you know?''

André made a great business of clutching at his chest and tottering to a nearby chair. "Good gracious!" he exclaimed wonderingly. "I do believe I am mortally wounded. Pierre, my only son, please, I beg you, take up the sword and defend your fallen sire."

Pierre lifted his hands to softly applaud his father. "Well done, sir," he complimented dryly. "Not that I am surprised you have chosen to retire to the fringes and leave me to make your explanations for you. My felicitations, Victoria, you remain as sharp as ever; even marriage to Patrick has not dulled your fire. Caroline," he continued, turning to face her. "I agree that you deserve some answers. However, before I tell you anything, I would ask that you promise you will listen very carefully to what I say, and then likewise promise to allow your friends to settle the situation for you while you remain out of harm's way."

Caroline very deliberately folded her arms across her stomach. "You'd have to be totally to let in the attic if you'd believe me, no matter if I swore those promises on a stack of Bibles piled high as the Tower of London," she pointed out reasonably. "Just get on with it, Pierre, please. Why don't you begin with Mrs. Merrydell, my dearest chaperone, if you need a place to start."

"All right, Caroline. I do begin to believe it would be performing a kindness to tell you something, so let me tell you what my father, through brilliant investigation, has learned—and then forwarded by way of discreet messengers almost daily to his son, who had been ruthlessly left behind here to act as resident nursemaid."

Pierre sat down familiarly at the bottom of the bed, as if the telling were going to take some time. "Mrs. Merrydell's meeting with you in the village was no accident," he began, much to Caroline's relief. "The entire incident was staged so that you would engage her services as chaperone, and the importuning dandy she beat heavily about the head and shoulders with her reticule was none other

153

than her son, Ursley Merrydell. I had recognized them both a week earlier walking together outside the inn in the village, as Father—who had discovered their presence before leaving for London—had prudently warned me against them. I had been keeping them under observation ever since, long before Mrs. Merrydell so graciously helped me by imposing her way into this house.''

"And you revealed *none* of this to poor Caroline,'' Victoria concluded quietly, shaking her head. "How infuriatingly typical of you, Pierre. At least André shared his knowledge of Mrs. Merrydell and Ursley with Patrick and me.''

Pierre slanted her a smile. "Explanations are so tedious, Victoria,'' he explained softly, but without apology.

"Ursley?'' Caroline exclaimed in disbelief, her mind whirling with this onslaught of information. "It is no wonder then that he grew up twisted, as if having Amity Merrydell for a mother were not inducement enough. Whoops!'' She put a hand to her mouth as Pierre frowned. "Please,'' she urged, "forgive my interruption. Go on.''

"Ursley was also the man Caroline first saw in the gardens—and the one who shaved the leather on her mount's cinch,'' Victoria interposed, her quick mind racing ahead to meet logical conclusions.

"One and the same, dear lady, I'm sure,'' André supplied from the corner. "We can only be thankful he is as incompetent as his mother is obnoxious—and that Caroline is an excellent rider who obviously knows how to take a fall.''

Caroline frowned, then voiced a protest. "But—but he couldn't be! The man in the cobbler's was not very tall, and quite thin, although still rather strong, in a wiry sort of way. The man in the garden was *huge!*'' Her frown deepened. "At least, I *thought* he was. Maybe it was his sack that was huge.'' She looked at Pierre. "And just maybe I was more frightened than I thought,'' she ended in a small voice.

"Now there's a revelation,'' Pierre told her, his smile taking any sting from his words.

Caroline immediately blushed to advantage, at least to Pierre's mind. "He's really such an unprepossessing little man. I feel foolish."

Pierre reached over to pat the hands that now lay in her lap. "We are all allowed to be foolish from time to time," he assured her.

She looked at him closely. "But not you," she said flatly. "You're always so composed."

She was amazed to see a slight hint of color invade his lean cheeks and immediately sensed he was thinking about his reaction to hearing that she had been hurt. Victoria had been correct; he must have been greatly overset. Caroline didn't know why, but it went a long way toward making her bruises less painful.

"We all have our moments, dear girl. Now," Pierre went on quickly, "to get back to the story as I know it. Father and I first became suspicious of the Merrydells when they installed themselves in the village a few days after you arrived at Standish Court. There was no reason for their presence, as the village is not exactly a social center, boasts no restorative waters, or can even be said to house an interesting historic ruin or two. So, armed with their names—as they signed the inn register with their true names, which was a mistake only dedicated bumblers could make—Father deserted us to set out for London, to conduct a small investigation."

"A very discreet yet intensive investigation," André amended carefully, "as I did not wish to expose my reasons for the questions I asked. I found no end of officials willing to speak to me about Mrs. Merrydell and her son, although I would beg Pierre not to soil your ears with all the details of the tales that I heard. I then traveled to dear Victoria and her Patrick, to enlist their aid as well."

"Do your best to appear flattered, Caroline," Pierre advised with a small smile. "Father doesn't go out of his way for people very often."

"Thank you, André," Caroline said dutifully. "Truly, I thank you all, for I have done nothing to deserve your interest in my dilemma. Now, with that out of the way, do you think, Pierre, that you could get on with it? I'm all but dying of curiosity."

Pierre obliged, for he knew that the explanation was rough ground and he'd rather get over it quickly. "Mrs. Amity Merrydell, although she is commonly known as Mrs. Amelia Chumley, Mrs. Agnes Forester, and Mrs. Agatha Terwilliger—there may be one other, although it escapes me for the moment—has made a moderately successful career of chaperoning less well-connected young ladies from the more remote regions of the country who wish to enter society. She inveigles herself into the unsuspecting family with false but glowing credentials, then introduces her son into the picture in the hopes of making a match with the young lady in question.

"When that ploy fails—and with Ursley cast in the role of hopeful swain, failure is all but a foregone conclusion—Mrs. Merrydell then steals what she can from her employer and departs for greener pastures. Bow Street has been looking for her for quite some time. Do I have it right thus far, Father?"

André rose from his chair to take up the story. "As far as I can say for now, it would appear that you, Caroline, were to be her next victim, only this time with a twist. Your guardian died while Mrs. Merrydell was in residence, leaving you alone, but not penniless. Unfortunately, you were also left with Mrs. Merrydell as your legal guardian, an error in judgment I prefer to believe was caused by your previous guardian's failing health."

"But that guardianship was to terminate with the arrival of your twenty-first birthday, when you would take control of your inheritance," Pierre added, watching her carefully for any signs of remembrance of the things they were telling her.

"Enter Ursley, the loving swain," Victoria concluded intelligently. "Mrs. Merrydell would have to marry you off to her son before you reached your majority, or else lose everything. She must have been sorely tempted. A few pieces of pilfered silver were nothing compared to having your entire fortune for herself."

Caroline raised her hands, wordlessly begging them to stop. "I may not know my own name, but I do know one thing—I would rather die than be married to someone with the name of Ursley Merrydell. And if that weren't enough, the prospect of having Amity for a mother-in-law would be ample inducement to cheerfully slit my own throat."

"Which, taking the thing a step further, leads us to the Merrydells' problem. If not marriage, then what?" Pierre asked silkily.

Caroline's mouth opened, forming a silent "Oh!"

"Yes, my dear girl; oh," André said kindly. "We feel certain you were on the run from your prospective murderers when you stumbled into my son's life. It is no wonder you lost your memory, as your memories include the death of your guardian and the prospect of falling victim to the Merrydells' greed."

Caroline shook her head, trying to take it all in. She knew she should be feeling sorrow for the loss of her guardian, but she couldn't. She had no memory of any guardian. Instead, she concentrated on the question of her appearance in Sussex. "But—but I still couldn't have gotten from Leicester to Sussex on my own. It's impossible."

"You weren't in Leicester, my dear," André put in quickly. "You were not thirty miles from here in a small, unpretentious town called Ockley, installed in a rented house to which the Merrydells had brought you, supposedly to recoup your strength after your guardian's death. After all, they could scarcely murder you in Leicester, could they? People would be too suspicious. If you refused to marry Ursley, they would simply arrange for you to have a fatal accident. It's all quite elementary, really, except that you must have discovered their plan and escaped, forcing the Merrydells to follow you here to finish the job."

Pierre, André, and Victoria exchanged glances while Caroline sat nervously plucking the bedcovers, deep in thought. Had they said too much, they asked each other silently. Had they said to little? Was this news too great

157

a shock on top of her recent accident? Would they jolt her into remembrance, or block out her past forever?

At last, when the three thought they no longer could stand the silence, Caroline spoke. "You *have* to know my name. You know too much *not* to know my name. Why won't you tell me?"

Pierre took her hand once more, squeezing it gently. "Only André knows the whole of it, and it is a secret he seems to delight in keeping. I know my father, and it is useless to press him, as he can be as close as an oyster when he wishes. Besides, Caroline, the doctor feels it would be unwise to tell you too much at once. He'd rather you remembered your past on your own."

"Doctor Burgess said that?" she questioned in disbelief. "He didn't seem to know enough about memory loss to make a judgment."

"No," Pierre agreed readily enough, "but the doctors Father consulted in London do, and it is their orders we have followed, and will continue to follow. We have given you some answers, some reasons for the attempts on your life. The rest will come back to you, Caroline, I'm convinced of it. Why don't you lie back now, and get some rest? All in all, you've had a busy day."

Pierre's oblique reference to the goings-on in her chamber brought Caroline's mind back to Mrs. Merrydell, and her eyes narrowed in sudden anger. "You *knew*," she accused Pierre, her voice tight. "You knew who she was, and what she wanted, and you let her stay here anyway? You let the woman who wants me dead sleep under the same roof with me—*and never told me?* Didn't you think I would be vaguely *interested?*" Her voice rose shrilly. "Just who in bloody hell do you think you are, to use me this way?"

Victoria coughed discreetly, catching André's attention, and the two withdrew from the chamber, leaving Pierre to face Caroline's rightful wrath as best he could. It might not have been the right thing to do, or even the fair thing, but it was, they silently agreed, precisely what Pierre deserved. After all, *he* was the one who had been assigned to protect her.

"They've left you," Caroline informed him tersely, having been forced to look away from his clear, unblinking gaze. "Like rats deserting a sinking ship, as the saying goes." Her bravado left her, and her lower lip began to tremble. "Oh, Pierre, how could you? I know I have been a bother to you, but were you so uncaring that you could install a murderess under your roof just to watch the sport as she stalked her unknowing quarry? Victoria told me this morning how you teased her husband with what you knew about that poor, confused man—Quinton's murderer—watching as he and Victoria ran about willy-nilly trying to find out what you already knew. Were you doing it again? Was this a diversion for you, a bit of sport? I thought—I thought you cared for me, if just a little bit."

Pierre shook his head, his all-seeing gaze never leaving her face. "Just like a woman, aren't you, throwing my past in my teeth. As Victoria has told you, I can be a wicked, wicked man. But, Caroline—my dearest Caroline—can you really believe I'd let anyone harm you? I allowed Mrs. Merrydell in this house because it was the one way I could watch her, and because I had hoped her presence might somehow serve to bring back your memory. You've never been in any danger from her. My only error was in underestimating the son's ability to outwit my grooms, which led to your accident yesterday. For that I should be horsewhipped. But please, Caroline, don't think your welfare is no more than a game to me."

Caroline drew a shaky breath, somehow knowing he was being more open with her than he had ever been with anyone in his life. He had not said he loved her, and she didn't really know if she was ready to hear those words from his lips. She only knew they had come a long way since their first meeting, that they had learned to trust each other at least a little bit, and that they were deeply attracted to each other. For now, with the cloud of her memory loss still hanging over her head, it was enough.

They had to take care of first things first.

She moved toward him a fraction. "What do we do now, Pierre? Do we call the constable? It's obvious Mrs. Merrydell's presence isn't going to jog my memory, so I would think she has outlived her usefulness. I want that woman and her son out of my life just as soon as possible."

Pierre leaned forward, placing a quick kiss on the tip of her nose. "That's my girl, pluck to the backbone. There's only one small, nagging problem. Ursley has somehow slipped his leash, abandoning his room at the inn and eluding the bumbling man I sent to follow him after his meeting with his mother this morning. It's so hard to get good help these days, you understand, what with the war. We do still have Mrs. Merrydell where we want her, but I don't want the mother without the son. He's a loose end I'd rather see neatly tied. Can I count on your help to flush him out of hiding?"

The idea of turning the tables on the Merrydells filled her with delight. "What do I have to do?"

He kissed her again, on the lips this time, and she was suddenly aware that they were, yet again, alone in her chamber and in a most compromising position. His arms held her gently, though she could feel the leashed strength of him against her, and she longed to experience what it would be like really to be held by him, loved by him.

She broke from his kiss, flushed and breathless, and pushed against the pillow. "Pierre? What do you want from me?"

He lifted his left eyebrow a fraction, causing her blush to deepen. "You tempt me, Caroline," he teased, "but I have promised myself to be good, so I will answer the question you thought you asked. What I want from you now, dearest girl, is quite simple—I want you to die for me."

Chapter Seventeen

It was a room rigged out for mourning the death of a beloved family member.

All the mirrors in the chamber had been shrouded with deepest black cloth, and the pictures denoting pleasant bucolic scenes or the smiling faces of various Standish forebears were all turned to face the wall.

The heavy, midnight-blue velvet draperies were pulled tightly across the wide windows, shutting out the light from the setting sun, and only a few softly flickering candles burned on either side of the black-crepe–hung bed that held the body of the late Caroline Addams—with two *D*'s.

All was quiet, hushed, until a high, piercing wail shattered the silence.

"Oh, my poor baby! My poor, poor baby!"

André came up behind the woman and took hold of her shoulders, his fastidiousness causing him to use only his fingertips in none-too-gently drawing her away from the doorway to Caroline's bedchamber. It wouldn't do to allow the harridan to enter and, most probably, cast her tall, angular body across the deceased in a distasteful display of grief.

"There, there, Mrs. Merrydell, attempt to get a grip on yourself, for all our sakes. Miss Addams was hardly your baby. It's not as if you knew her all that well, much as I am gratified to see your deep concern."

Mrs. Merrydell dabbed at her rouged cheeks with a lace-edged handkerchief, cruelly pushing a corner of the linen into one eye in order to manufacture a credible tear before she turned to face André. "It's not just that, dear sir. I was in charge of her welfare." She moaned disconsolately. "I should never have allowed her to go out for that ride yesterday. I knew, after all, that she was suffering some terrible scrambling of the brainbox—misplacing her memory, that is. She had no business on a horse, did she, sir? Oh, why did she have to die?"

"You mustn't blame yourself, my dear lady," he told her bracingly. "It was an accident, nothing more." André looked past the woman into the chamber, to where Caroline lay on top of the bedcovers, neatly dressed in a white lawn nightgown that covered her from neck to toes, her arms crossed gracefully over her breasts, a small sprig of wildflowers held in her clasped hands. Pierre had added that last bit, and André privately agreed it was a nice touch, although he much preferred roses.

"And just as we all thought she had rallied," he lamented sadly. "She was fine one moment this morning, sipping some of the lovely tea you made for her with your own hands and promising that she would even join us at table for dinner. And then—*pouf!*—she was gone, snatched from us in the first sweet flower of her youth, her last breath sighing from her body even as my son watched in horror. Ah, the pity of it, Mrs. Merrydell, the bleeding pity of it. And now we will bury her, hide her away in the cold, cold ground, without ever knowing her true name."

Mrs. Merrydell flung herself heavily into André's arms. "Oh no! *Dear* sir, no!" she cried in what might have been grief but could just as easily have been panic. "You cannot allow that to happen. Surely you must wait—in the chance someone may come to identify her! Surely someone will come!"

So that was it! "Someone" would come. That had been the part of the mother-to-son conversation Pierre had missed. André allowed himself a small smile. "It is a comforting thought, Mrs. Merrydell, and I *have* been placing advertisements in all the newspapers with just that hope in mind, since the very beginning. But in truth, madam, how long can we wait? After all, the weather is still warm.

Excuse my indelicacy, but one cannot keep a dead body about indefinitely in the heat, can one? Of course," he added, as if thinking aloud, "there is always the icehouse, I suppose."

"Yes! That's it! Put her on ice!" Mrs. Merrydell exclaimed excitedly, then quickly lapsed once more into loud sobs of anguished grief.

André looked over the woman's shoulder and thought he could see Caroline's chest rising and falling slightly in silent mirth. "There, there, Mrs. Merrydell," he soothed, rolling his eyes in disgust at her blatant overacting. Disengaging himself from her convulsive grip, he hastened the weeping woman down the hallway to the stairs before a giggling corpse could give the game away.

"I'm bored." Caroline pushed out her lower lip in a pout and crossed her arms over her chest as she sat in the middle of her bed, a deck of cards carelessly scattered across the satin coverlet. "And I'm hungry!"

Victoria, who had just entered the chamber, closed the door behind her and locked it securely. *"Shhh!"* she warned, a finger to her lips. "I'm supposedly the only person in this room who is capable of speech. For all our sakes, keep your voice down, Caroline."

She reached into her pocket to pull out an apple. "Will this do for now?" She tossed it to Caroline, who deftly caught it with one hand. "I'm only sorry I couldn't bring you my own uneaten dinner on a tray. I am convinced it was delicious, for everyone else ate their fill, even the grieving Mrs. Merrydell—who had two helpings of dessert—but I took one bite and thought I was going to disgrace myself by becoming ill right at the table."

"An apple, and not a big one at that. André brought me part of a nice meat pie from the kitchens when he stopped by earlier, but all you could find was an apple? Ursley had better show up soon to identify my remains or I'll starve to death." Caroline rubbed the apple against the satin coverlet, then bit into it, pushing the bite to one side of her mouth to add, "I'm sorry you're feeling ill, Victoria—it's

163

the baby, isn't it? I know I'm being demanding, but Susan, my maid, is being less than useless.''

"She seemed quite competent to me," Victoria said, frowning.

Caroline smiled. "That was before I died. She won't come anywhere near me since laying me out. She said I gave her the creeps, talking and laughing all the time she was putting this white powder on my face and hands to make me look bloodless." She turned her face this way and that. "What do you think, Victoria? Do I look properly dead?''

Victoria ignored this question, and sat down in the chair beside the bed, rapidly fanning herself with her handkerchief. "It's positively airless in here with all the windows shut. You may be enjoying yourself, Caroline, but I can tell you that—thanks to the unremittingly obnoxious Mrs. Merrydell—I have about reached the end of my tether. She insists on pestering us to be allowed to keep a vigil over your body, and breaks into hiccupping sobs every few minutes, just to let us all know how grievously she is suffering. I escaped up here just now because I was sure I would do her an injury if I had to remain in her encroaching company another moment.''

Caroline was instantly contrite. She slid from the high bed to pour Victoria a cooling glass of water from the pitcher that stood on a stand in the corner. "Poor thing," she said sincerely, handing her friend the glass before crawling back onto the coverlet and recovering her apple. "The woman is dreadfully in the way, isn't she? Pierre should be forced to handle her, not you.''

"Pierre?" Victoria laughed. "He's too busy arranging for the removal of your perishable mortal remains to the icehouse in the morning. Not that he plans to actually put you in storage, as it were, but only to hide you elsewhere in the house, as it is difficult to have you laid out here, where Mrs. Merrydell might be able to sneak in and see your supposed corpse gnawing on a chicken leg. Pierre is convinced that Ursley will appear tomorrow as if on cue to view the body—clutching one of André's advertisements in his hand, no doubt, and claiming you are his long-lost fiancée."

"No doubt," Caroline agreed coolly as she laid the apple core in a small dish on the nightstand. "Ursley Terwilliger is a toad, but he has always been an extremely punctual toad. As I recall, it is his single redeeming virtue."

The water glass dropped to the floor unheeded, to splinter into a hundred pieces. *"Caroline!"* Victoria exclaimed in sudden excitement, her fatigue, and even the slight queasiness she had been feeling lately whenever confronted by food, forgotten. "It's working, just as the doctors said! It's above everything marvelous! All you needed was a start, some gentle nudging. You're beginning to remember!"

Caroline put a trembling hand to her suddenly aching forehead and stared at her friend in wonder, not really seeing her but concentrating on a picture that was floating in the forefront of her mind. "I can see him, Victoria . . . sitting at the head of a long dining table . . . pushing food down his skinny throat as fast as he can. How dare he sit there? He doesn't belong there."

"Who does belong there?" Victoria prodded in a fierce whisper, leaning toward the bed. "Who belongs there, Caroline?"

"Caroline?" Caroline covered her eyes with her hands, trying to recapture the image that had splintered and disappeared. "Oh, it's gone. It's gone." She looked at Victoria, her huge eyes burning with tears in her powdered, too-white face. "I—I don't remember. Who—who is Caroline?"

"Oh, my dear Lord," Victoria breathed in horror, wishing she could kick herself for her loose tongue. "You've forgotten who you are *now!* This couldn't be what is supposed to happen. Just stay there, my dear, and try not to worry. I must get Pierre at once."

Caroline was looking at her strangely, just as if she had never seen her before that moment. "Pierre? Who is Pierre? I know no one by that name." She shook her head, then winced at the pain the movement caused.

Victoria's eyes opened wide behind her spectacles, and she knew she was gaping at Caroline, her mouth at half-mast. "You—you don't remember Pierre, either?"

"Pierre? No. Silly French name. And who are you? Did you tell me your name? Oh, my head. It hurts terribly. It's so strange. I never get the headache. Oh, well, I can't think about that now. What were we talking about? It hurts to think, just like that evening I tried champagne when I wasn't supposed to and could barely remember how to walk. I'll ask my questions again later. Would you mind if I were a poor hostess and lay down for a time? It helped enormously when I drank the champagne. Grandfather will surely be delighted to entertain you while I rest. We have so few visitors here at Abbey House, you know."

Her heart pounding with mingled dread and excitement, Victoria dared to try pushing Caroline a little farther. "Yes, of course," she agreed swiftly. "I don't mind at all, Miss— oh, dear, what a scatterbrain I am! Please forgive me but, like you, I have always had such a difficult time with names. Now I seem to have forgotten yours."

Victoria held her breath as she waited for Caroline to answer.

The girl was already lying against the pillows, her knees drawn up high against her body, one hand tucked beneath her cheek. Her eyes closed, she murmured quietly, "Please don't apologize. My name is Catherine. Catherine Halliford. But dearest Grandfather, he always calls me Caro."

It was after midnight.

Pierre paced the floor of his father's study like a caged animal, once more like the dark, brooding panther to which his father had once so aptly compared him.

Everything was wrong, he decided, pounding his fist into his palm. From start to finish he had bungled the affair, and bungled it badly.

It was his fault that Caroline—no, *Catherine;* he had to

begin thinking of her as Catherine—was lying upstairs, deeply asleep or unconscious, he did not know.

He should have turned Amity Merrydell and her idiot son over to the constable the moment he had decided they were out to harm Catherine. Never mind that he had possessed no proof; never mind that all he could have told the constable was that the two were suspicious merely because of their presence. But no, he had been content to wait, believing himself superior to anything they might try, any rig they might run.

"Arrogant," he said aloud as he walked to the drinks table to pour himself three fingers of port. "You're so damned arrogant, Standish. I don't know how you stand yourself, you're so bloody perfect."

And if he couldn't have had the pair of them tossed into gaol, he should have taken greater care with Catherine. He had been placed in charge of protecting her, while his father had gone haring off in search of her true identity. It had been a simple job, elementary actually, something any moderately intelligent ape could have accomplished without undo effort.

But, no, he had to botch that as well, not once, but twice. "London society has dulled your wits, Standish," he told himself, tossing off the port. "You've degenerated into the very worst sort of man, becoming nothing but a toothless drawing-room ornament."

Even Sir John Oakvale, that featherbrain who had more hair than wit, could have done better than he had, and with one badly manicured hand strapped behind his back! It was a disgrace, that's what it was, and Pierre knew that if he lived to be one hundred, he would never forgive himself.

Pouring another drink, he continued with his mental self-flagellation.

The day Ursley had accosted Catherine in the cobbler's shop—that should have been the day the man drew his last breath. He should have throttled the miserable little worm, choked him until his eyes bulged from their sockets, then tossed his carcass in the dirt and had his harridan mother transported in chains to the other side of the world.

But no, he had been too smart to do that, too enthralled with the supposed brilliance of his own schemes to consider that he might be playing a dangerous game with Catherine's physical welfare.

Even when she fell from her horse, he had chosen not to act, but merely played the spy, watching Amity Merrydell and her son as they met at the bottom of the gardens to discuss strategy. Merely capturing them was too mundane, too expected. He was going to dazzle Catherine with his ingenuity, his fancy footwork, by tripping the Merrydells up at their own game.

The fine French crystal goblet hit the cold stones of the fireplace and exploded with an unsatisfying, splintering crash.

If he had been too thick, too impressed with his own brilliance to act before, why hadn't he called a halt to the game when his father had returned home with definite evidence that the Merrydells meant to kill Catherine? Yes, there had been the business about Ursley escaping the eye of the man sent to watch him, but how dangerous could that puppy be without his mother to direct him?

His reluctance had been only another excuse in an endless string of excuses that allowed him to continue playing the game.

Now Catherine's overburdened mind had snapped beneath the strain, sending her into a dark, confused world where she knew her name but had lost all recollection of him, the man who loved her beyond life itself. What an evil justice!

He hadn't been able to look at Victoria, meet that intelligent woman's eyes when she had come to tell him what had transpired in Catherine's bedchamber. He had fled from the room, leaving his father and Victoria to whisper between themselves, and had hidden here in this study, where his frustrated pacing was fast wearing a hole in his father's carpet.

The only thing worse than going back over his many

mistakes was thinking about the young woman lying in the room above him. His supposed redeeming Good Deed. Would this sleep she had slipped into ease Catherine's confusion, so that when she awoke—if indeed she ever did awake—she would remember everything—her past, her present, and, he prayed with all his being, some slight knowledge that she may have planned for a future that had him in it?

Their future together. His heart squeezed with pain at the thought. How had he come to this—he, Pierre Claghorn Standish, who had been heart-whole for so long? When had it happened? When had his concern for Catherine turned to love; when had his very natural attraction to a beautiful young woman grown into passion?

He remembered her kiss, the feel of her soft warmth pressed against him, wordlessly telling him things he had no right to ask. Even in that he had behaved abominably, advancing on her when she was off-balance, her mind confused, her body injured. He was a cad—worse than a cad. He didn't deserve her.

If only she would waken and look at him with recognition in her beautiful wide eyes. If only she would waken whole, with all her memories intact. He would let her go then, knowing she would be all right. He didn't deserve her love, and wouldn't press his suit anymore.

He stood sightlessly staring down into the fireplace at the second wanton destruction of his father's crystal in two days, then gave a short, self-mocking laugh. "Who do I think I'm kidding? I can't do that. I *won't* do that."

"Prattling to yourself, my son?" André said from the doorway. "Bad sign, that. Perhaps your time would be better spent in prayer."

Pierre turned to face his father, looking at him from beneath half-closed lids, his dark eyes unfathomable, his face an emotionless mask. "Prayer? You're becoming damned moral, Father. It doesn't suit you."

"Just as the sackcloth and ashes you're wearing fit you extremely ill," André responded, causing his son to wince. "I asked for a softening tint of humanness, a smidgeon of humility. I did not ask for maudlin self-pity. Poor Victoria has just stumbled off to her bed near tears, unable to reconcile herself to your lack of fighting spirit. You've been a bitter disappointment to her, you understand, as she had begun to think of you as unflappable."

A tic began to work in Pierre's cheek. "Enjoying yourself, Father?"

André sat down behind his desk, crossing his legs. "Oddly, Pierre, I'm not. I believe I like your deliberate arrogance much more than this uncharacteristic sentimental self-condemnation. It certainly isn't doing Catherine much good, and on top of everything else, it's dashed boring to watch."

Catherine. Mention of her name brought Pierre's head up, and he stared at his father, who was looking back at him levelly, a small smile on his lips, his brows raised a fraction, as if waiting for his son to speak. "Father, I—"

"Yes, *mon fils?*" the older man purred.

The corners of Pierre's mouth slowly curved upward as, with a deep, flourishing bow to his sire, he threw off his despondency. "My congratulations. You're still the master, *mon pére*. Now, if you'll be so kind as to excuse me, I have a pressing matter to attend to before our expected visitor descends on us."

"You're going to Catherine?" André questioned softly as his son walked toward the door. "I'm very pleased."

Pierre stopped, his hand on the latch, but did not face his father. "I don't give a tinker's curse for your pleasure, Father. Between us, *pleasing* ourselves has led to more heartache than happiness. It's my *salvation* I seek now."

Chapter Eighteen

He used his key to enter Catherine's darkened bedchamber, locking the door behind him while consigning any thoughts of impropriety to the devil. This time was his, his and Catherine's. He would brook no intrusions from the outside world.

Walking over to the bed, he looked down at her sleeping form. She looked totally at peace, with the world and herself, a slight smile curving her lips as if she were dreaming of some fond memory.

Was it a memory of him? He doubted it.

Pierre frowned, noticing the white powder that still marred the perfection of her beloved features. It was another reminder of his stupidity, and he felt an overwhelming urge to have it gone. He extracted his handkerchief and sat down on the edge of the bed, using the clean linen to softly wipe away the traces of powder.

This was love. For the first time in his life he understood why his father had been so happy, and why he had retired from society when his beloved wife had died. He understood Patrick's desperation when confronted with Victoria's plan to ferret out Quennel Quinton's murderer, for the need to protect one's beloved was an all but overpowering emotion.

And how Pierre loved his Catherine. His love had stripped him of all arrogance, all confidence, and even, for a time, all common sense. His father had been wrong. Completing a good deed would not make Pierre human. Only love could do that.

So intent was he on the performance of his task, so

involved was he with his thoughts, that Catherine took him completely by surprise when she opened her eyes and looked directly up into his tear-streaked face.

"Pierre," she whispered, her own eyes filling with tears. "Please don't cry."

"Catherine!" he breathed hoarsely as she reached to pull him down to her. "You remember me. Oh, thank God! My dearest love! You remember me."

"I love you, Pierre," she said simply, those four words, spoken so matter-of-factly, thawing once and forever all the ice that had for so long surrounded his heart.

It was ten o'clock in the morning, and they were all gathered around a heavily laden tea tray in the drawing room, Mrs. Merrydell having earlier been securely locked in a storage room by Pierre, who had kept his resolution not to play at conspirator any longer. Now he sat beside his beloved on the settee, dressed in his impeccable black and white, looking well rested and ready for action.

"Grandfather Halliford had been ill for a long time, not that I wasn't devastated by his death," Catherine told her interested audience. "It was his greatest wish that I have a Season in London, which is why he hired Mrs. Merrydell as my chaperone and mentor although, as we've already established, Grandfather and I knew her as Agatha Terwilliger.

"I disliked her on sight, and really didn't wish for a Season, but Grandfather was adamant. He may have been naught but a simple, successful manufacturer of shoes—a rich upstart with machine oil beneath his fingernails, as he described himself—but his granddaughter was a full two generations from the smell of the shop! He was quite a man, my grandfather, and the reason my language is, as you all have noticed, sometimes unladylike."

"Never unladylike," André interrupted from his position against the mantelpiece. "Your grandfather's generation, male and female both, were much freer with their speech than people of polite upbringing are supposed to be today. For myself, I find your lapses honest and re-

172

freshing. But I must be quiet. Please continue with your story, Catherine, my dear."

Catherine thanked him for his kind words and went on, "You can imagine my distress when I learned Mrs. Ter— Mrs. *Merrydell* was to be my guardian. We had no living relatives and I suppose Grandfather, knowing I was soon to reach my majority, saw no harm in it."

Victoria set down her empty teacup and leaned forward slightly in her chair, the better to see Catherine, for she had purposely left her spectacles on her dresser that morning. "You must have been terribly overset. But your grandfather sounds to have been a wonderful man, and I am happy to hear you do not hold his ill judgment against him. How was he to know the Merrydells' dastardly plans for you?"

Catherine grimaced. "Marriage to Ursley had been their first intention, but I wasn't having it. I was walking in the gardens when I overheard them discussing the proper way to dispose of me," she told Victoria as Pierre reached over to squeeze her hand.

"I had removed my slippers so that I could creep closer and hear everything without giving myself away with my footsteps, when I stepped on a dry branch—and the race was on." She chuckled, remembering the way she had run barefoot into the forest, Ursley doing his best to follow her in his ridiculous high-heeled shoes. "I lost him easily enough, but I had no money, no shoes, no idea where I was, and no one to turn to for assistance. In the end, Ursley found me again, and I would have been well and truly caught if Pierre hadn't come along. Of course, I rather wish I hadn't been so clumsy as to trip over a rock and hit my head in my effort to capture his coachman's attention. All I could think about was getting back to Abbey House. Even now, it isn't a pleasant memory."

"Many a man would have broken under such strain," André assured her. "I don't wish to press you further, Catherine, but one thing still troubles me. How did you come by the cloak?"

Catherine turned to grin at Pierre, who grinned back,

having already heard the story as the two of them, lyi
side by side on her bed, had talked through the night.
stole it, of course," she quipped. "Somewhere there i
gentleman who will never again leave his cloak behind
his curricle when he visits a country inn for luncheon. T
only thing I feel sorry for is stealing that lovely pie fr
some good farm wife's windowsill. But I did have to e
didn't I?"

Victoria got up and went to squint through the wind
overlooking the drive at the front of the house, her th
visit to the window in the past half hour. "I'm just hap
it has all turned out so well, especially after that little sc
you gave us last night, Catherine. First you lost your pa
then you misplaced your present—it is good to have all
you with us this morning."

"Hear, hear!" André echoed, lifting his teacup in
toast. "Still looking for my man to return here from f
away Leicester, Victoria?" he asked as he replaced
cup on the mantel. "Perhaps if you sent a maid for y
spectacles."

The young matron flushed becomingly and shot An
a quelling look, just as the sound of a horse approachi
the house at a rapid clip filled the room. She pushed as
the thin draperies to look out over the drive, gave a sm
girlish squeal, and ran for the foyer.

Catherine looked after her friend, frowning in con
sion. "What on earth—"

Pierre gently pushed her against the settee. "My w
have been dulled, have they not, Father, that I have
guessed before now? Your man, the one who was to ma
the final confirmation of Catherine's identity, is none ot
than my good friend, Patrick Sherbourne. I should ha
known he wouldn't allow estate business to keep his a
tocratic nose out of my affairs. He's waited too long
some well-earned revenge."

A few moments later, the Earl of Wickford and
countess entered the drawing room arm-in-arm, and Pie
and Catherine rose to greet them as André, looking pleas
with himself, watched from a distance.

174

"Pierre, you sly old dog!" Patrick called, extending a hand to his friend. "What's this I hear about cupid's arrow having got you at last? It couldn't happen to a more deserving man. And this is Catherine," he continued as Pierre took his hand and shook it. "Such a little thing to cause such a great upheaval. You have my deepest thanks, Miss Halliford. I understand from my wife that you have succeeded in penetrating this fellow's dark soul and bringing it into the sunlight. Heaven knows I've tried and failed a dozen times or more."

"Perhaps you didn't possess the correct tools, my lord," Catherine answered, coloring under Patrick's interested scrutiny.

Patrick threw back his head and laughed out loud. "She's witty as well as beautiful, Pierre," he told his friend. "The question remains, however—what are you, a confirmed bachelor, going to do about it?"

Slipping an arm around Catherine's shoulders so that he could pull her close to him, Pierre answered, "As I once told you, my friend, understanding the workings of a woman's mind is a lifelong study. I begin to believe that I shall enjoy that study, and all that goes with it, immensely."

André, having heard another horse approaching up the drive, cleared his throat as he pushed himself away from the mantelpiece. "I hesitate to interrupt this heartwarming, truly affecting reunion, gentlemen, but it appears we are about to have another visitor."

"Ursley," Catherine said at once, one hand involuntarily going to her throat. She looked up at Pierre, her eyes wide. "I can almost forgive him, for he was naught but his mother's tool, but do I have to see him, Pierre? It's silly, I know, but his face will bring back so many unpleasant memories."

Pierre's expression hardened, his dark eyes going strangely flat and colorless. He had promised her he would capture the man with as little fuss as possible and have him carted off to gaol with his murderous mother. He had

175

promised, but now seeing the fear on Catherine's face, he regretted that promise.

Catherine saw the reluctance in his face, correctly interpreting how he felt. Pierre was unused to following orders, as he had been forced to do throughout most of this strange adventure, and his every instinct cried out for him to finish the project by marking its conclusion with his own, very individual stamp.

She bit her bottom lip, realizing that, although she loved him when he was open and vulnerable, as he had appeared to her a few moments last night when his tears had betrayed his deepest emotions, and she loved him excessively when he was being tender, as he had been with her all through the night, she loved him best of all when he was being arrogant, self-assured, and totally in control of a situation he had, in his own inimitable way, engineered.

She didn't say a word, but he knew what she was thinking. His left eyebrow, the one she alternately despised and adored, rose almost imperceptibly as he looked down on her and breathed quietly, "Caro?"

Catherine smiled brilliantly, then slipped from beneath his encircling arm to grab Victoria's hand and lead her toward the door to the morning room. "Come, my friend. We're dreadfully in the way right now, as the boys wish to play, and we wouldn't want to rob them of their sport."

"I like her, Pierre," Patrick declared, grinning. "I like that little girl more than I can say." He rubbed his palms together in anticipation of what he was sure to be some jolly good fun. "Now, what do you want me to do?"

Pierre turned toward the door to the foyer, absently adjusting his snowy cravat with one steady hand. "Just follow my lead, my friend, and I'm sure you'll pick it up in no time. Father? Are you with us?"

André spoke from the chair he had positioned himself in, his legs crossed negligently at the ankle, his handsome face looking as bright and lively as his son's. "Need you ask *mon fils?* Let the farce begin."

* * *

"Mr. Ursley Terwilliger, sir," the loyal Hartley announced as he stood, rolling his eyes, just inside the open door.

Ursley entered the room in a great rush, brandishing a copy of one of the London newspapers, just as Pierre had prophesied, only to collide with the butler as that unfortunate man turned smartly on his heel to return to his post before—from the fierce expression on his face—he gave Terwilliger a pop on the nose.

Ursley's mother, had she been present, would have cuffed her son on the ear for his clumsiness, and that lowering thought instantly filled him with a firm resolve not to blunder again. "Watch where you're walking, you dolt!" Ursley blustered, rudely pushing the old man to one side and thereby giving his audience one less reason to love him. "Where do you have her?" he demanded hotly—following the script his mother had written for him—while rushing up to where Pierre stood watching him, idly stroking the crescent-shaped scar on his left cheekbone. "Where do you have my darling Catherine?"

Pierre peered owlishly down at Ursley, his dark eyes raking the smaller man from head to toe and obviously concluding the man was lacking—something or other, exactly what Ursley couldn't be sure. He only knew he had been judged and found wanting.

"*Ter*-williger. Terwilli-*ger?* Ter-*will*-iger!" Pierre mused aloud, then shook his head sadly. "No, I'm afraid not. I can't say as I recall the name. But then, I meet so many people. Have we been introduced?"

"Yes . . . no! . . . that is . . ." Ursley floundered into silence. Where was his mother, damn her black soul to hell anyway! She promised she'd be here, to guide him through this. His shifty gaze shot around the large, sunlit room. She hadn't told him the father was going to be here as well. The only thing that could be worse than one Standish was *two* Standish's. And who was that grinning fellow over there, for crying out loud? *Mama!* he cried silently. He wanted his mama!

"Terwilliger," Patrick drawled silkily, walking up to

stand beside Pierre, the two tall, handsome, immaculate
dressed men making Ursley feel small and more unlov
than ever. "I once knew a Terwilliger on the Peninsu
Wellington had him hanged from a tree, for looting
believe. He was a poor dresser, as I remember him, w
always looked as if he had made his own trousers. A
relation, old man?"

Ursley ran a finger inside his suddenly too-tight coll
"No!" he exclaimed quickly, guiltily removing the fing
"No relation at all. I—I'm here because of this," he
plained, holding out the newspaper that was folded ba
to expose André's advertisement. "Having read it m
carefully, I believe your unknown young woman to
none other than dearest Catherine Halliford, my missi
fiancée."

André, his quizzing glass stuck to his eye, rose to w
fully around Ursley's now noticeably trembling body. "
reads," he said, as if to assure himself he had heard arig
Turning to Patrick, he repeated, "He reads! I would
have thought it. It must have been the waistcoat. I've
ways wondered about the mental profundity of gentlen
who prefer pink satin, haven't you, Patrick?"

The earl could barely suppress his mirth. Marriage v
wonderful, but there was nothing like a bit of good f
with one's male friends to brighten a day. "I'll rese
my answer until I've inspected my own wardrobe, sir,
you don't mind," he answered congenially. "But I th
we are being sidetracked by this discussion of Mr. T
williger's intellectual prowess. He seems to be inquir
about your houseguest, the woman you called Carol
Addams. I think he is convinced she is his long-lost love

Pierre raised a hand to his mouth, feigning shock. "(
dear! Patrick, do you really think so? Now here's a
lemma. How can I do this tactfully?" He turned to le
at Ursley, who was perspiring quite freely in the c
room. "Could you perhaps describe to us the young la
in question, Mr. Terwilliger?"

Describe her? Ursley was nonplussed. His mother s
they had the dratted girl laid out upstairs. Why could

he just tippy-toe up there and take a quick peep in at her? Something was wrong; he could feel it in his bones. The bitter taste of failure was a familiar one, and it was stinging him now, deep in the back of his throat. "Describe her, you say. Yes, well, *um*," he began hesitantly, "she was short. Yes, that's it, short—and dark."

"Dark skin?" Pierre pressed him.

Ursley shook his head. "Dark hair, light skin." He held out his hand at shoulder level. "And—and short."

"Pretty?" Pierre asked, unearthing his enameled snuffbox and offering some of his personal sort to everyone save Ursley.

The smaller man frowned, trying to decide if Catherine was pretty. She was presentable enough when she kept her mouth shut, he supposed. "Pretty," he answered, nervously clearing his throat. "Look—if I could view, I mean, if I could just *see* her—"

Pierre shut the snuffbox with a loud snap that instantly had Ursley thinking of the trapdoor falling open beneath the gibbet. "That's impossible, sir." He took hold of Ursley at the elbow. "Not that I don't believe you, you understand. Our Caroline Addams is most certainly your Catherine Halliford."

"So—so what's the problem?"

"Perhaps you should sit down," Pierre suggested, his voice tinged with sympathy. "I fear I have some bad news."

Well, it was about time! Suppressing a relieved smile, Ursley allowed himself to be led to a chair, looking over his shoulder at Pierre as that man walked round to stand behind him, almost as if guarding him. "Bad news? Your advertisement said she had lost her memory. Don't tell me it's even worse than that? You—you aren't going to tell me that she's *dead*, are you?"

And that, as Patrick was to tell Victoria later, was when the bottom fell out of Ursley Terwilliger-Merrydell's dreams of wealth.

"Dead? My good gracious, no. I shan't tell you anything of the kind, Mr. Terwilliger," Pierre assured him,

laying one hand heavily on his shoulder as Ursley ma~
to rise.

"She—she's not?" Ursley squeaked, twisting in t~
chair to look up at Pierre.

"No, she's not. She's in amazingly good health, as ~
matter of fact," Pierre assured him. "I will, however, t~
you that your Miss Halliford is also the most fickle ~
women, and not worthy of your obvious devotion."

"Oh, don't dress it up in fine linen, my son," And~
broke in. "It won't make it any easier for the poor fello~
in the long run."

Ursley's head whipped around to look at the older Sta~
dish. "It—it won't?"

"No," Pierre said, sighing. "It won't. I'm sorry to ~
the bearer of such sad tidings, Mr. Terwilliger, but yo~
Miss Catherine Halliford eloped last night with my val~
Duvall. They will be well on their way to Gretna Gre~
by now, I imagine. I shall miss him, for he did have t~
most wonderful way with a cravat."

Ursley Merrydell, looking as if he had been poleaxe~
slumped in his chair as if all his bones had turned to mus~
Patrick turned on his heel to head for the drinks tab~
fearing his expression would give the game away. Pie~
was in top form this morning; he had to hand it to t~
man, especially as this was an impromptu performanc~
Patrick almost pitied Ursley, for even such a dolt as ~
must know now that the game was up.

Patrick had been half correct in his assessment. Ursl~
was a beaten man—yet he was also wiser. He looked ov~
to where André Standish was lounging against the ma~
telpiece, and could read his fate in that man's dark eye~

He didn't have to see Pierre Standish's face, for he co~
feel that man's heavy hand on his shoulder. He wonder~
randomly where they had put his mother, and how ma~
of them it had taken to subdue her, and he wondered wh~
Catherine Halliford would enter the room, very mu~
alive, to point an accusing finger and confront him w~
the full gravity of his intended crime.

All in all, it was the most profound bit of wondering

which Ursley had ever subjected his brainbox in his lifetime, and he was beginning to feel the dull throb of a headache approaching behind his eyes.

He made another, albeit halfhearted, attempt to rise. "Yes, well, these things will happen, I guess. I'll go now, I think," he mumbled, then felt a renewed surge of hope as Pierre removed his hand, allowing him to get to his feet.

"You do that," Pierre purred, smiling at him in a way that made Ursley feel the man could have killed him without so much as blinking an eye. "I think you should go very far away, please, *Mr. Merrydell,* and never, ever return. Your mother will not follow you, if that news cheers you, as she'll be otherwise occupied for quite some time. Do they still have the women beat hemp at Bridewell, Father, do you suppose?"

Patrick whirled in astonishment. Was that compassion he heard in Pierre's voice? "You're letting him *go?*" he asked, incredulous. They had done all this, only to let the man go? "You've got to be kidding!"

But André, walking across the room to lay an arm across his son's shoulders, only smiled and said proudly. "Please, dearest Patrick, don't sound so amazed. My son is a very human sort. It becomes him, don't you think?"

Epilogue

London was anxious for the start of the fall Little Se son, with stragglers daily arriving back in the city fr their house parties or hunting parties or periods of ju cious retrenching after spending a poor spring season the gaming tables.

If there was a little added fillip to the buzz of goss that was once more making its rounds through the *h ton*, it could be traced to the presence of André Standi in their midst after an absence of more than six yea Previously one of the darlings of the *ton*, it was alrea as if he had never been gone. No evening was comple without him, no hostess a success unless he graced h party.

Yet even more exciting, although at the same time pressing, at least to the eligible young ladies and hope mamas in their midst, was the appearance of Pierre Sta dish, his smiling bride on his arm. The town had been on its collective ear with the news of the marriage of t unfathomable Pierre to his gorgeous young heiress, a everywhere they went necks craned so that people co observe the couple as they strolled through drawing roo or went gracefully down the dance.

The Earl and Countess of Wickford were also in tow even though the dear countess was increasing, a fact t could be overlooked, as they were hosting André Standi at their mansion. As a matter of fact, as a show of supp to the young countess, more than a few matrons were ne sporting spectacles whether they needed them or nay.

Indeed, it was showing all the signs of being an extraordinarily festive Little Season.

André, out for a stroll in the park, his oddly endearing blond page skipping three paces behind him, couldn't have agreed with Society more. As he walked in the cool afternoon sunshine, his walking stick idly twirling between his agile fingers, he called over his shoulder without turning around: "Master Holloway, I implore you, although I appreciate your happiness at being once more in London, try not to whistle like that. You're unnerving the horses as they pass by."

"Yer gots it, Whitey, right an' right!" Jeremy Holloway responded gaily, with his usual disregard for André's consequence. He smoothed his hands down the front of his new jacket, wondering if they would be stopping at the guv'nor's house for dinner so that he could show this latest mass of beauty to Frenchie. He'd be that proud, Frenchie would, for the two of them had become bosom chums since they had helped to rout the Merrydells. It also helped the fledgling friendship considerably that they no longer resided beneath the same roof.

Jeremy looked down the path, his eyes brightening. " 'Ey, Whitey, ain't that the guv'nor an' 'is missus comin' up on that rattle an' prad?"

André looked ahead, to see his son and his daughter-in-law approaching in a shiny midnight-black high-perch phaeton, Catherine handling the spirited greys between the shafts with an ease that marked the true whipster. He stopped on the path and planted his walking stick, waiting for them to draw up alongside.

"Good day to you, Father," Pierre called, tipping his hat. "I see you have gotten your Good Deed yet another new suit of clothes. You'll spoil him, you know."

"Master Holloway is completely unspoilable," André responded carelessly. "Besides, as I recall, he was to be *your* Good Deed. Catherine was mine, until you usurped her." He winked up at her, for she already had been informed as to the whole of the events that had led to Pierre's willingness to accept her and Jeremy as his responsibilities.

Putting her arm through her husband's, Catherine looked into his eyes and drawled cheekily, "Jeremy may be uncorruptible but I, on the other hand, simply *adore* being indulged. What do you have to say to that, my dearest husband?"

With a look so soft and loving in his dark eyes, a melting look that would have astonished anyone who had ever faced the not-yet-reformed Pierre Claghorn Standish across a green felt table or a dewy green dueling ground, he responded quietly, "I say I have every intention of indulging you shamelessly all the days of our lives."

And then, shocking and titillating the passersby, he leaned down quite deliberately and kissed his wife square on the lips.

André smiled, whether in memory of his own love or in celebration of his son's happiness only he knew. With a tip of his hat to the oblivious pair, he resumed his walk, calling over his shoulder, "Master Holloway! A whistle if you will—and damn the horses!"

AVON REGENCY ROMANCES

by

KASEY MICHAELS

NEW!—
THE PLAYFUL LADY PENELOPE

75297-2/$2.95 US/$3.95 Can

THE QUESTIONING MISS QUINTON

75296-4/$2.95 US/$3.95 Can

A precious clue leads to a number of suspects of Victoria's father's murder...including the rogue who had stolen her heart.

THE MISCHIEVOUS MISS MURPHY

89907-8/$2.95 US/$3.95 Can

For once, Tony Betancourt, Marquess of Coniston, had met his match in wit and mischief, and soon might win a bet—but forever lose his heart!

AND DON'T MISS—
THE SAVAGE MISS SAXON   89746-6/$2.95 US/$3.95 Can
THE BELLIGERENT MISS BOYNTON

77073-3/$2.95 US/$3.95 Can

THE LURID LADY LOCKPORT   86231-X/$2.95 US/$3.95 Can
THE TENACIOUS MISS TAMERLANE

79889-1/$2.95 US/$3.95 Can

THE RAMBUNCTIOUS LADY ROYSTON

81448-X/$2.95 US/$3.95 Can

Avon Paperbacks

Buy these books at your local bookstore or use this coupon for ordering:

Avon Books, Dept BP, Box 767, Rte 2, Dresden, TN 38225

Please send me the book(s) I have checked above. I am enclosing $_____
(please add $1.00 to cover postage and handling for each book ordered to a maximum of three dollars). Send check or money order—no cash or C.O.D.'s please. Prices and numbers are subject to change without notice. Please allow six to eight weeks for delivery.

Name _____

Address _____

City _____ State/Zip _____

KM 8-89

*If you enjoyed this book, take advantage
of this special offer. Subscribe now and . . .*

GET A *FREE*
HISTORICAL ROMANCE

—— NO OBLIGATION (a $3.95 value) ——

Each month the editors of True Value will select the four best historical
romance novels from America's leading publishers. Preview them in
your home Free for 10 days. And we'll send you a FREE book as our
introductory gift. No obligation. If for any reason you decide not to keep
them, just return them and owe nothing. But if you like them you'll pay
just $3.50 each and save at least $.45 each off the cover price. (Your
savings are a minimum of $1.80 a month.) There is no shipping and
handling or other hidden charges. There are no minimum number of
books to buy and you may cancel at any time.

send in the coupon below

Mail to:
True Value Home Subscription Services, Inc.
P.O. Box 5235
120 Brighton Road
Clifton, New Jersey 07015-1234

YES! I want to start previewing the very best historical romances being published today. Send
me my FREE book along with the first month's selections. I understand that I may look them
over FREE for 10 days. If I'm not absolutely delighted I may return them and owe nothing.
Otherwise I will pay the low price of just $3.50 each; a total of $14.00 (at least a $15.80 value)
and save at least $1.80. Then each month I will receive four brand new novels to preview as
soon as they are published for the same low price. I can always return a shipment and I may
cancel this subscription at any time with no obligation to buy even a single book. In any event
the FREE book is mine to keep regardless.

Name _____

Address _____ Apt. _____

City _____ State _____ Zip _____

Signature _____
          (if under 18 parent or guardian must sign)
Terms and prices subject to change.   75668-4